THE WINTER
WORM BUSINESS

It was probably the end of his career, Leroy thought.

THE WINTER WORM BUSINESS

PATRICIA REILLY GIFF
Illustrated by LESLIE MORRILL

A Yearling Book

Published by
Dell Publishing
a division of
Bantam Doubleday Dell Publishing Group, Inc.
666 Fifth Avenue
New York, New York 10103

The trademark Yearling® is registered in the U.S. Patent and Trademark Office.

ISBN: 0-440-49259-9

Reprinted by arrangement with Delacorte Press

Printed in the United States of America

One Previous Edition

December 1989

10 9 8

CW

A special thanks to
Roger Ricco
who knows about
the mountains and the river
and who never minds
answering my questions
about them.

For
Olga Jean Litowinsky
with thanks
and love

THE WINTER WORM BUSINESS

CHAPTER 1

Leroy Wilson shoved his bedroom window up and stuck his head out.

It had snowed. Finally. And on a Saturday too. He had been waiting for weeks. Only a half-inch lay on the ground but buckets more were coming down.

At one end of the street was the river. Today it looked cold and almost black. Leroy stuck his head out a little farther and looked at the houses. Counting his own, there were seven on each side. All the roofs were covered with a thin layer of white. At the other end of the street where the houses ended, High Flats Road snaked upward toward Hubbell Mountain.

Leroy could see Tracy Matson lying on her front lawn across the road. She was wiggling her arms and legs back and forth. He guessed she was trying to make an angel in the snow. Instead she was digging her heels into the grass and making a muddy mess.

She looked up and caught him sticking his tongue out to catch a snowflake.

"I thought you were dying, Leroy Wilson," she yelled.

Leroy ducked his head in, shut the window, and sank down on the floor to lean against the radiator while he put his sneakers on.

It had been a great week. He had been in bed with a bad cold ever since Monday and had watched all the quiz shows on television. And to top it off, his mother promised him a big surprise this weekend.

It was probably a pony. He had been begging for one since he was seven years old and had just about given up.

Tracy Matson would be furious when she heard he had gotten one before she did.

He wandered downstairs to get his breakfast.

"Leroy." His mother's voice floated in from the kitchen. "I think Mrs. Grant is coming with the mail. Will you get it?"

Leroy put his head out the door as Mrs. Grant came puffing up the front walk.

"I guess you're pretty excited," she said as she handed him the mail.

Leroy nodded. It had to be a pony if the whole town knew about it.

"I'd be thrilled if I had cousins my own age who were coming here to live."

"Cousins?" Leroy repeated, thinking that if Mrs. Grant had cousins like his, she'd probably want to drown them right in the river.

"Yes," Mrs. Grant said over her shoulder as she went back down the steps. "I guess you're pretty excited about Mitchell."

Leroy left the mail on the table in the living room

and staggered back up to his bedroom. He sat down on the floor in front of the radiator. He couldn't believe it.

It was probably the end of his career as the smartest fifth grader in the Thaddeus Lowell School. All Aunt Louise ever talked about was how smart Mitchell was.

Not that Leroy cared too much about being at the top of Mrs. Claycomb's honor roll.

What he did care about was what everybody would say when they got a look at his genius cousin Mitchell Everhart and Mitchell's eight-year-old sister, Elaine.

Everyone always said that he and Mitchell could be twins. Same hair, same eyes, same teeth, and same nose. Except that Mitchell always had his finger in his. Besides, Mitchell talked too fast. He always had a little saliva in the corners of his mouth. And when he wasn't talking he was chewing on his fingernails. Elaine, his little sister, had a thumb problem. She had sucked her thumb until it had calluses all over it and it had pushed her teeth out so she lisped when she talked.

Everyone in school would be laughing all over the place when they found out Leroy was related to a pair of drooling idiots.

Splat. Leroy jumped. In back of him a clump of wet snow hit the window. Tracy Matson again. That girl was such a pain. She was a rotten reader but she was the best fisherman in the fifth grade and she could throw a ball as well as he could.

Leroy stood up and leaned his forehead against the icy windowpane. "What are you trying to do," he yelled, "break the darn window?"

3

"What about the worms?" she shouted back. "And we need some more leaves. By the time we get this thing all set up, the ground will be frozen five feet down."

"Hold your horses a minute, will you?" he screamed. He pulled down the shade so he wouldn't have to look at her crazy brown hat, which covered her eyebrows and most of her carroty braids.

He could still hear her yelling about worms and leaves as he clattered down the stairs, muttering. A person couldn't even think around here in peace.

His mother and father were in the kitchen. "Rice Krispies or Raisin Bran?" she asked.

"Pancakes," Leroy answered, still frowning.

"It's my day off," his mother said. "How about some toast?"

Leroy shook his head and helped himself to a bowl of cereal.

"Well," said his mother. "Are you ready to hear about the surprise?"

"I don't think so," Leroy said.

His mother beamed at him. "You won't be stuck with Tracy Matson much anymore," she said. "And you won't have to wait for Richard to come all the way over here from Windsor."

Leroy put his head down and looked carefully at his Rice Krispies. He had never noticed how many little holes there were in each one.

"Your very dear cousin"—she drew the words out slowly—"Mit-chell E-ver-hart and his sister, E-laine, are coming here to live. Right down the street at Mrs.

Clausson's boardinghouse." She frowned. "Aunt Louise is getting a divorce, so she just packed everything up to come here."

Leroy poured some milk in his cereal and packed down the Krispies.

"Best of all," his mother continued, "Aunt Louise is going to give piano lessons. I told her to sign you right up."

"Argh," Leroy said into his cereal.

His mother cocked her head to one side. "I thought you wanted to take piano lessons."

Leroy stuffed a bunch of Krispies into his mouth. "I did," he said as soon as he could talk. "But now I want to take the guitar." He strummed an invisible guitar, stamping his foot and bobbing his head in time with the imaginary music.

His father laughed. He stood up, still drinking the last of his coffee. "Well," he said, "I'll let you two settle this. Right now, I've got to get in some overtime." He kissed Leroy's mother good-bye, took his lunch pail off the counter, and shrugged into his jacket.

After he had gone, Leroy looked up at his mother. "Besides," he said, "who wants to take lessons from Aunt Louise? She's a big pain."

"Leroy!" his mother said. "That's not nice. And I've already told Aunt Louise. We can't disappoint her now."

"I've got to find my boots," Leroy mumbled through his cereal.

"You've been sick in bed all week," his mother said. "I don't know whether you should be out in the snow."

5

"I'm all better," he answered. "It doesn't even hurt when I swallow. Look." He swallowed as hard as he could.

"All right," his mother answered. She looked doubtful. "Your boots are in the storeroom, I think."

Leroy took a couple of mouthfuls of cereal, then put the bowl under the table for his new dog, Fumbles. Fumbles, a big black dog with a long feathery tail, put one paw on Leroy's knee, then bent down to polish off the rest of the cereal.

Leroy stood up and went out to the storeroom to find his rubber boots. They were covered with spiderwebs and junk.

Ten minutes later, red-faced and sweaty from trying to pull the boots over his sneakers, he threw the boots against the wall as hard as he could and grabbed his jacket.

Outside it was freezing. By the time he came around to the front of his house, his sneakers were wet through. His feet would probably be frostbitten and purple by the time he got back in. Good. Maybe his mother would realize that he wasn't a baby anymore and needed a pair of work boots just like his best friend, Richard.

Tracy Matson was still waiting for him in the middle of High Flats Road. "Listen, Leroy," she yelled. "If you think you're going to get half the money from this business, you'd better put a little more effort into it. I'm sick of doing all the work. I was stuck with those fifty worms all week."

"I thought we had sixty," Leroy said.

6

Tracy waved her hands around. "Lost ten somehow." She looked a little worried. "I hope they don't turn up under my mother's feet somewhere."

From the other end of High Flats Road there was the sound of a car. Leroy looked over his shoulder. A blue Camaro. Just like Aunt Louise's.

"Wonder who that is," Tracy said.

"Some idiot probably," Leroy muttered. "But we don't have time to stop now. The ground is really getting covered. If we're going to get another fifty worms this morning, we'd better get to it."

CHAPTER 2

Leroy led the way past his house, across the field.

"What do you mean, 'some idiot'?" Tracy asked.

Leroy shrugged. "Do you think I keep track of every car that comes down High Flats Road?" he asked.

As they approached the bridge that spanned the river, he stopped short. "Forgot the shovel," he said, annoyed.

"I could—" Tracy began.

"No," said Leroy. He thought of Mitchell, who was probably lurking around somewhere to tell everyone in the town of High Flats how much smarter he was than Leroy Wilson, his first cousin, who looked just like him. "I'll get it myself."

He stopped for a moment to look at the river. "Not freezing yet."

"Not one bit," Tracy agreed. "But don't you worry, Leroy. Mr. Kirk will be able to drive his tractor across the whole thing before you know it. About a million ice fishermen will be falling all over us."

"That is," Leroy said, "if we have enough worms."

He trudged back across the field and headed toward

his garage, keeping his head as low as he could. He spotted Elaine standing in the middle of the street, thumb in her mouth.

She spotted him too. She took her thumb out of her mouth. "Your mother's looking all over the place for you, Leroy," she screeched. "She says you're going to catch your death of cold going out without your boots. You'd better . . ."

Leroy slammed the garage door behind him. He pulled the shovel off the hook, opened the back window, and pushed the shovel out ahead of him.

He landed in the snow with a thud. He could still hear Elaine screaming. "Mitchell," she was yelling, "I found Leroy for you. He's right in the garage."

Leroy picked up the shovel and took off for the river. When he reached the bank, he slid down to the rocks where Tracy Matson was already digging with a sharp-edged stone.

"You forgot a jar too, I bet," Tracy said.

Leroy sighed.

"Don't worry," Tracy said. She held up a plastic Clorox bottle. "I washed it out and stuck in some dead leaves and things so the worms'll feel right at home until we get them into their cage in my cellar." She held the bottle up to one eye and squinted into it. "Got two already."

Leroy shook his head. "We should have thousands. Should have been out here every day."

Tracy pulled off her hat and shook the snow out of it. "Don't blame me for that, Leroy." She jammed the hat back on her head. "You certainly got a lot of mileage out of one cold. Stayed home all week, missed two tests, and I ended up with the worms in my cellar for the second week in a row. If my mother—"

"Listen, Tracy," Leroy said. "I had a fever. A hundred and one. Besides, I'm going to take the worms off your hands today."

He began to dig. In ten minutes he had dropped fifteen worms into the Clorox bottle. He was also ready to quit. He had forgotten his gloves; his sneakers and socks were soaked; and he felt as if his back would cave in if he leaned over the shovel any longer.

But Tracy Matson was still going strong. She had no gloves on either. And it looked as if her boots had about forty holes in them. But she was hopping around from one rock to another, turning them over, pulling out worms faster than a greased weasel. At the same time, she kept telling him to hurry up.

Leroy felt like clunking her with the back of the shovel.

"Look," she said. She broke off a stalk of goldenrod that was in her way. "There's always a grub in these." She snapped open the tiny pod on top. "Not bad for ice fishing." She shook her head. "But who wants to clump around on the riverbank, knee-deep in snow, to gather them?"

"Why don't we get some now?"

"That's your whole trouble, Leroy. You don't know enough about fishing. A decent fish doesn't snap up a piece of dead bait. He wants it alive. You pick those grubs, they'd be deader than doornails by the time ice fishing time comes. No," she said. "We'll stick to worms."

Above them a stone rolled down the bank. Leroy looked up.

Mitchell Everhart stood there. He had a brand-new pair of work boots, the kind with about a thousand holes for laces, better even than Leroy's friend Richard's from Windsor. Mitchell was wearing gloves. Leather ones.

"Need any help down there?" Mitchell called.

Tracy straightened up. "Who's that?"

"Nobody," Leroy muttered.

"He looks just like you, Leroy," Tracy said.

"Mitchell C. Everhart," Mitchell said. "Do you need any help?"

Tracy squinted up at him. "Tracy Matson. Where'd you come from?"

Mitchell pointed to Leroy. "I'm his cousin," he said.

Leroy gritted his teeth.

"How come you didn't tell me your cousin was here?" Tracy asked.

Leroy didn't answer.

"Well, what about it?" Mitchell asked. "Do you need some help?"

Tracy looked at Leroy. "What do you think?"

Leroy put his shovel down and rubbed his back. "How many worms do you think we have now?"

Tracy picked up the bottle, squinted into it, and rolled it around gently. "I'd say about forty."

Leroy shook the snow off his shoulders. "Fifty plus

"Need any help down there?" Mitchell called.

forty is only . . . um, ninety. And at a nickel apiece when the ice fishing starts, that's about five dollars and forty, no sixty . . ."

"Four dollars and fifty cents exactly," Mitchell broke in.

Tracy looked at Mitchell with interest. "You did that in your head?"

"No," Leroy said. "He just whipped out his invisible pad and pencil."

"Very funny," Tracy said. She turned back to Mitchell. "Can you divide four dollars and fifty cents by three?"

"Certainly," Mitchell said, chomping on his fingernail.

"No good, Tracy," Leroy said furiously. "If you think I've been breaking my back so that Mitchell can get rich selling worms to the ice fishermen, you're crazy."

Mitchell looked disappointed for a moment. Then he slid down the bank and landed on a rock in front of them. "Sorry," he said, "I can't join your business anyway."

"Why not?" Tracy asked. "We can use all the help we can get." She glared at Leroy. "Some of us aren't really working hard enough."

Leroy turned his back on them and began to shovel. If Tracy persuaded Mitchell to get into the worm business with them, then he was going to quit. That's all he needed: Mitchell on top of him all the time with his computer brain and his chewed-up fingernails.

"Can't," Mitchell said. "I'm starting a business of my own."

Leroy turned around again. "What business?" he asked in spite of himself.

"Guide."

"Guide?" Tracy repeated doubtfully.

"You know," Mitchell said. "Show the city people around when they come up here to fish this winter." He looked at the river. "There's ice fishing, isn't there? And the hunters. I can take them away from snakes and stuff. Mountain lions."

Tracy looked impressed. She nodded slowly. "No mountain lions," she said absently.

Leroy dropped his shovel. It was more than he could bear. "Guide," he screamed. "You've just arrived yourself. You haven't been here a half an hour." He looked at Mitchell with disgust. "Wipe your mouth off, will you? You've got spit all over yourself."

Mitchell looked off into the distance and waved his hand around. "Give me two days here in the wilderness," he said, "and I'll know it as if I've lived here all my life." He looked at Tracy. "I'm like that," he said. "If I want something, I go after it. Study it. Know what I mean?"

"Wilderness," Leroy snorted. "What are you talking about?"

"Just a figure of speech," Mitchell said. "Don't get excited." He wiped his mouth.

"You could put up signs," Tracy said, "out by the highway and over in Windsor."

"Windsor?" asked Mitchell.

"Signs?" Leroy asked.

"The next town," Tracy said. She looked at Leroy. "Advertising." She blew on her hands and jammed them into her pockets. "HUNTING AND FISHING GUIDE," she said in a loud voice. "AT YOUR SERVICE." She cocked her head to one side. "REASONABLE RATES," she said after a minute. "That's what all the advertisements say."

"Not bad," Mitchell agreed. "Hey, I just had a great idea."

"Tracy," Leroy said, "it's really getting cold. We'd better get the rest of the worms and bring this mess indoors, before the Clorox bottle is a hunk of ice."

"It's not all that cold." Mitchell wiped some snow off the top of his brand-new-looking leather hat. "As I was saying, maybe the two of you would like to join in my business. Tracy could help me with the actual guide work. And Leroy . . ." Mitchell stopped to consider. "Leroy, you could . . ."

Leroy swallowed. "Tracy and I have our own business going here, Mitchell."

"Don't be silly, Leroy. We can go into both businesses at the same time. Why don't you just finish up with the worms here, and Mitchell and I can go up to my house. Get the signs started. After all, Leroy, you can see by the snow, winter's really here."

She and Mitchell clambered up the bank. As they hurried across the field, Leroy heard Tracy say, "Leroy is just dying for a pair of work boots like yours, Mitchell."

Leroy stood looking at the river. Suddenly everything was still. It seemed as if there weren't another soul in the whole world. Nothing but the snow falling softly.

Leroy gulped. He watched the river for a minute more. He noticed that there was a small skim of ice around the edge of the river in the mullein weeds. Then he picked up his shovel and started to dig again.

CHAPTER 3

Monday morning was a disaster. Leroy had just about squeezed his feet into his old, cobwebby boots when his mother appeared in the storeroom and handed him his lunch bag.

It was tuna fish again. He could smell it right through the bag. So would everyone else on the bus.

"It's all set," his mother said. "Aunt Louise promised you could be her very first pupil."

Leroy sighed. If only Aunt Louise wasn't such an air brain, he'd really like to take piano lessons. He could just see it. Tracy would sit there, watching him play something really hard, his hands crossing back and forth over the keys . . .

He looked up at his mother. "How long?"

His mother blinked. "What do you mean?"

"How long until I'm better than Mitchell?"

His father appeared in the doorway. "You know, Leroy, Mitchell and Elaine, and even Aunt Louise, are having a hard time right now. It isn't easy when a family splits up. I hope you're going to be nice to them. Include them in things."

Leroy ducked his head. "Yeah, I guess so."

He waited until his father had gone back into the kitchen. "How long?" he asked.

"Well, if you practice every day, about an hour . . ." His mother looked at the ceiling. "A couple of years, I guess."

Leroy staggered back into the storeroom. "A couple of years. Forget it. I'm taking the guitar."

His mother frowned. "I don't think Aunt Louise knows how to play the guitar."

Leroy nodded grimly. "I figured that."

"If you practice hard," said his mother, "you might get a pair of work boots for your birthday next month."

Leroy shook his head. "Not worth it."

His mother put her hands on her hips. "I don't want to hear another word about it. You are going to take piano lessons as soon as Aunt Louise is unpacked and settled in. We can't disappoint her."

Leroy slammed out the back door. It had snowed all day Sunday. The snow was piled high on the side of the house and in the driveway. He plowed through a drift, dusted himself off, and crossed his front lawn.

He could see everyone milling around the bus stop at the end of High Flats Road. Tracy Matson was throwing snowballs at Mitchell Everhart. And Elaine was standing by herself, sucking her thumb and crying. The only one missing was lucky Poopsie Pomeranz, the second grader who lived across the street.

Leroy looked across the field past Poopsie's house. The bus was nowhere in sight. Maybe he'd have time to check the ice in the river.

Carefully he put his books and lunch on top of some hard-packed snow at the side of the road.

He raced down High Flats Road toward the river. In back of him Tracy Matson shouted, "You're going to miss the bus, Leroy."

He looked over his shoulder. Across the field he could see the yellow bus in the distance. He ran faster.

When he reached the river, he slid down the bank. For a moment he stared at the river's edge. Small chunks of white floated along in the water and the reeds looked as if they had been dipped in glass.

The river was icing up. Finally.

He turned and scrambled up the bank and tore down the road. He stopped to scoop up his books, then he barreled for the bus stop.

He made it just in time. Tracy had managed to climb in first, as usual. She was sitting behind Herbie, the bus driver. Mitchell swung in next to her.

Leroy shrugged. He never sat next to Tracy anyway. He always sat in the back and saved a seat for his friend Richard.

He found his favorite spot, right over the heater, the seat that had a long ragged tear in it. He kept an extra pencil and a dime deep inside the rip under the cottony stuff of the seat in case he needed them. Now he wiggled his finger into the opening to make sure his stuff was still there.

Elaine, sniffling and sucking her thumb, plumped herself down beside him. Leroy looked up as she took her thumb out of her mouth long enough to say, "What are you doing, Leroy?"

Leroy bounced back against the seat as Herbie pressed down on the gas pedal and the bus started up the road to Hubbell Mountain.

"You can't sit here," Leroy whispered to her. "Get away." He looked toward the front. It was a good thing there were still only a few kids on the bus.

"Sit somewhere else," he whispered again. "You can't sit here."

"Can so." Elaine stuck her thumb in her mouth.

"You're in Richard's seat."

Elaine didn't even bother to take her thumb out of her mouth. "I'm your cousin," she said in a muffled voice and began to cry again.

Leroy gave her a little push.

Elaine planted her feet firmly on the floor and held on to the seat in front of her. "Mitchell won't sit next to me," she wailed, "and I don't know anybody."

Leroy slapped his hands on his legs in frustration. He would have liked to plant his foot on Elaine's back and push her right up to Mitchell in front of the bus.

Instead he leaned his forehead against the steamy glass window and stared at the snow as the bus rumbled across Hubbell Mountain. Every few minutes he could hear Elaine sniffle.

"Stop crying," he said.

"Why?"

Leroy shrugged, trying to think of a reason. "Too bad Poopsie isn't here," he said finally. "She's in second grade too."

Elaine sniffled. "Where is she?"

"At her grandmother's. Probably watching a thousand TV shows every day."

"How come?"

"She was twirling around on her stoop the other day. You know, doing ballet. Then she twirled herself right off the stoop into the bushes. Broke her leg. She's got a big cast."

"Why is she at her grandmother's?"

"Her mother has to work. She can't take care of her all day."

Elaine didn't say anything so Leroy looked out the window again.

At the bottom of the mountain, the bus slowed down. It passed the sign that said: WINDSOR, POPULATION 326, and slid to a stop in front of Richard, his brother Barry, and some other kids who lived in Windsor.

The door opened and Richard lumbered to the back of the bus. Leroy guessed he had forgotten all about his diet again because he had a huge bag of lunch under his arm.

He grinned at Leroy, showing two broken front teeth. Then he saw Elaine.

"Out," he said. "Now."

Elaine started to cry again.

Leroy sighed.

"Move," Richard said, "before I throw you out."

"Move," Richard said, *"before I throw you out."*

Elaine scrambled to her feet and slid into an empty seat across the aisle. "Leroy . . ." she began and started to cry.

Leroy looked away. There was so much noise on the bus now, with kids yelling back and forth, that he could hardly hear her.

As Richard plopped himself into his seat and tore open his lunch, Leroy dug into the side of his seat again until he felt the pencil and the hard roundness of the dime he was looking for. He left them there in case he needed them tomorrow.

With one elbow Richard nudged Leroy. "Who's that tear bag?" he asked as he pawed through a bunch of knobby little packages wrapped in Baggies.

Leroy shrugged.

Richard pulled out a pack of raisins, held it out to Leroy, then popped a couple of raisins into his own mouth.

"River's really icing up," Leroy said so that Richard would forget about Elaine.

"I might come over on my bike some afternoon this week," Richard said, chewing, "and take a look at it."

"Great," Leroy said, then remembered Aunt Louise and the piano lessons. He wondered how long it would take her to unpack. "Well, I don't know . . . I'm not sure which day . . ."

"Why not? Got something better to do?"

Leroy pictured himself at the piano in Mrs. Clausson's boardinghouse. All the boarders would be sitting there, rocking, with nothing better to do than watch him. Worse yet, Mitchell would be lurking around in a corner, finger in his nose, smirking.

Leroy shuddered.

"The thing is, Richard," he began, "I have to take . . . My aunt . . ." No. He couldn't tell Richard that. Richard would probably think he was crazy for taking piano lessons.

Richard gave him a poke. "Who's that up in front with Tracy? Look at that neat jacket."

"New kid," Leroy answered shortly. "Mitchell Everhart."

As Richard craned his neck to get a better look at Mitchell, the bus pulled into the schoolyard and came to a stop.

In front of Leroy, everyone stood up and scrambled for the door. Leroy was the last one out. Except for Elaine. He turned and spotted her still sitting in the back of the bus, crying.

Her nose was red, and stringy pieces of hair were plastered to her wet cheeks. She looked revolting.

He felt like leaving her there. Let Herbie the bus driver take care of her, he thought. Or one of the teachers.

He hesitated, then went up the aisle toward her. "What's the matter with you?" he asked irritably.

But Elaine didn't answer.

He reached for her books, picked her lunch up from the floor where it had fallen, and grabbed her by the arm. "Come on," he said. "You're going to be late."

Reluctantly, Elaine got to her feet and followed Leroy out of the bus.

As they crossed the yard, one of the third graders pointed toward them. "Leroy's got a girl friend," she shrieked. "Leroy's gonna get married. Ha, ha, ha."

Everyone turned to look at them.

Head down, Leroy maneuvered Elaine across the rest of the yard and through the heavy door into school.

CHAPTER 4

Leroy dropped Elaine off in front of the principal's office. Mitchell was there ahead of them, talking to Mrs. Butts, the school secretary. Half of Mitchell's breakfast was scattered around his mouth, and his chin was all damp.

Leroy felt like gagging.

"Hold on a minute, Leroy, and I'll walk up with you," Mitchell said. He smiled at Mrs. Butts and jabbed a finger toward Leroy. "My cousin."

Leroy said "Hi" to Mrs. Butts. He noticed that Mitchell had saliva all over his chin. "I have to go upstairs, Mitchell," he said, backing out of the office. "I'll be late."

"Don't worry, Leroy," Mrs. Butts said. "Mitchell can go right up with you. Tell Mrs. Claycomb he's all registered."

Mrs. Butts smiled at Elaine. "You must be Mitchell's little sister. That was nice of Leroy to take care of you."

Elaine smirked at him. "You're my cousin. Right, Leroy?"

"Right," Leroy mumbled.

"And my best friend too. Right?"

Leroy gritted his teeth. He marched out of the office with Mitchell right behind him.

Upstairs, Mrs. Claycomb had already started. Leroy could see her through the little window in the classroom door. As usual she was rushing back and forth across the front of the room. She was as skinny as Tracy Matson and had red hair too. Today she had on a pair of plaid slacks and a fuzzy yellow sweater.

She frowned a little when she saw Leroy open the door but then she beamed when she saw Mitchell standing there. "A new student," she said. "I knew something good was going to happen today." She bustled Mitchell into an empty desk near the front of the room.

Mitchell looked around as he unzipped his jacket. "Very nice," he told Mrs. Claycomb. It sounded as if he were the principal.

"Thank you," Mrs. Claycomb said, looking a little surprised. "You can hang your coat on any of the empty hooks in the back."

She went to the blackboard. "I should have erased this last week," she said to the class and pointed to a fat Christmas tree she had drawn there early in December. She erased it and began to draw what looked like a bunch of white lumps but were probably snow-covered mountains.

"Yes," she said as she drew in a boy on a sled, "some people think that January is a boring month, but I find that there are lots of things to do. Ice skating and sleigh riding and . . ." She hesitated. "And . . ."

Leroy leaned back. Mrs. Claycomb liked to make long speeches about how wonderful everything was. He sneaked his library book halfway out of his desk and began to read. The book was all about ice fishing. The best place to fish, said the author, A. J. Abermarle, was right at the spot where an underground stream fed into a river. Fish would be coming from an icy cold area into a warmer spot, hoping to find growing plants.

Leroy looked out the window at the mountains and thought about a bunch of fish swimming around. He couldn't picture them hoping for anything. Also it was too late for him to find an underground stream in the river because A. J. Abermarle said that summer was the time to do that. Leroy had never even thought about ice fishing once last summer.

He wiggled around in his chair. It had started to snow again. He stood up in his seat to see a little better, then sank back as Mrs. Claycomb looked in his direction. He looked at the clock. It was only twenty minutes after nine. He wondered what it would be like to stay home every day for weeks like Poopsie and watch the quiz shows on television.

"And so," Mrs. Claycomb was saying, "for January we are going to concentrate on all the things we have to be thankful for."

Mitchell raised his hand.

Mrs. Claycomb smiled at him. "Yes, Michael?"

"Mitchell. M-i-t-c—"

Mrs. Claycomb drew her eyebrows together. "I know how to spell Mit—" she began.

"I was thinking, Mrs. Claycomb," Mitchell cut in. "We could write a sentence every day . . . you know, 'I'm thankful for . . .' and then we could read them out loud. Kind of find out what everybody had to be grateful about."

Leroy sat up straight. Just the kind of freaky thing you could count on Mitchell to suggest.

Mrs. Claycomb's eyebrows smoothed out. "That is a terrific idea, Mitchell." She looked around at the class. "It would be better, though," she said mildly, "not to interrupt me when I'm speaking."

Mitchell nodded seriously. "I was thinking I can probably tell you about a lot of interesting things we did in my other school."

Mrs. Claycomb looked as if she didn't know what to say. "That's fine," she answered finally. "In the meantime, suppose we all take out a piece of paper and write down what we have to be thankful for today." She turned back to the board and began to make a bunch of chalk dots for snowflakes.

In the next row Richard was eating pretzels. His cheeks were bulging. He held the open bag out across the aisle.

Leroy took a quick look at Mrs. Claycomb but she still had half a board to dot so he reached in the bag and took a few pretzels.

Richard swallowed and leaned over a little closer.

"That kid looks a little like you," he whispered. "But I think he's going to turn out to be your average nut case."

Leroy nodded, hoping that Richard wouldn't find out that the nut case was his cousin.

"We ought to tell him about the mountain monkeys," Richard continued.

Leroy swirled his tongue around a pretzel. It was the salty kind. He could have eaten about a hundred. He looked toward the front of the room at Mitchell. Mitchell was sitting there picking his nose. "I guess so," he said.

Just then Mrs. Claycomb stopped dotting the board.

Leroy pulled out his notebook. At the same time, Mitchell raised his hand. Mrs. Claycomb nodded at him.

"Do you know what I have to be thankful for?" he asked Mrs. Claycomb.

She shook her head. "Why don't you read what you've written?"

Mitchell picked up his paper. "I am thankful," he said in a loud voice, "that I am in a good class with a great teacher and my best friend and cousin, Leroy Wilson."

Leroy swallowed the last pretzel, then he slid down in his seat. Everyone was looking at him. He looked at Mitchell. Mitchell's face was still a mess.

As Mitchell sat down, a note wrapped around an eraser hit the top of Leroy's desk with a clunk. He opened it, trying not to let the paper crackle. It was from Tracy Matson.

"We ought to tell him about the mountain monkeys."

Dear Leroy,

You have to take the worms home today. Don't forget anymore. If my mother finds them, she will throw them out.

See me later. I will tell you how to take care of them.

T.M.

Leroy looked at the note, annoyed. He picked up his pencil and scrawled across the bottom: I KNOW HOW TO TAKE CARE OF WORMS AS WELL AS YOU DO. Then he passed the note to Richard. "Give this to Tracy," he mouthed.

Richard nodded. "I didn't know he was your cousin," he whispered apologetically. "Forget I said that about the mountain monkeys."

Leroy leaned forward so he could look across Richard's desk to Tracy's. She was bent over a piece of yellow oak tag, writing something with a fat red Magic Marker.

He hunched up in his seat to see what she was writing.

T. MATSON AND M. EVERHART
WILDERNESS GIDES

Leroy could feel his mouth open wide. Then he pulled a piece of paper out of the binder, ripping the little holes. He pulled a box of reinforcers out of his desk and picked out two of the little white circles. He

licked them carefully and stuck them on his paper.
Wilderness guides. He couldn't believe it.

He picked up a ballpoint pen and wrote:

I am thankful there are only twenty-four days left
in January.

CHAPTER 5

On Thursday it was too cold for anyone to be sitting on Mrs. Clausson's porch. The three boarders must be inside, sitting in the living room, waiting for the big activity of the day: listening to Leroy's first piano lesson.

Leroy squared his shoulders. There was no way out. He waved to Elaine, who was playing in the snow. Then he climbed the three front steps and walked across the porch, his footsteps sounding loud on the gray wooden floor.

Aunt Louise must have been hanging around waiting for him, because she came out the front door before he even had a chance to knock. She was stuffed into a silky purple dress and had long pink beads around her neck.

"My dear Leroy, come in," she said. "I'm sure you'll be playing Beethoven in no time." She led the way down the hall into Mrs. Clausson's living room.

Only one of the boarders was sitting there. Mr. Twillig. He was living at the boardinghouse now that he had retired from the lumbering business. He had no family so he said he liked being at Mrs. Clausson's where people were always coming and going.

Mr. Twillig looked over the top of his newspaper and nodded at Leroy. Leroy nodded back, staring at Mr. Twillig's hair. It was gray and curly and it hung down almost to his shoulders. He had told Leroy one time that his hair was the best thing about himself so he let it grow as long as he could so everyone would notice it.

Mrs. Clausson's piano took up almost one whole side of the room. Hanging on the wall over it was a big round mirror. And in front of it was a long bench. Aunt Louise sat down at one end of the bench and motioned for Leroy to sit at the other end.

"You're my sixth pupil," she said. "There's Elaine and Mitchell, of course, and three children from Windsor. All of them have been taking piano lessons for quite a while. The piano teacher in Windsor moved out last month though. Fortunately for me."

As Aunt Louise paused for breath, Leroy nodded absently. He wondered what Richard was doing this afternoon.

"Now let's begin," said Aunt Louise. "We have a lot of catching up to do."

She stretched her arms out in front of her and made claws of her hands. "Curl your fingers over the keys like this," she said.

Leroy made claws too. Just like Dracula, he thought, admiring the way his hands looked. He made them look even more scary.

"Very nice, Leroy," Aunt Louise began, then drew

Leroy made claws. Just like Dracula, he thought.

in her breath. She was staring at his hands. "One thing I really must insist on," she said, "is im-mac-u-late hands."

Leroy curled his hands over the piano keys a little more to hide his fingernails.

Behind him, Mr. Twillig rattled his paper.

Quickly Leroy glanced up at the mirror to see if Mr. Twillig was paying attention, but he was buried behind his newspaper.

"Perhaps," said Aunt Louise, "you could use Mrs. Clausson's bathroom down the hall and get them clean."

Leroy slid off the piano bench and went down the hall to the bathroom. He spent a long time soaping his hands with Mrs. Clausson's strawberry soap. It made his hands smell terrible.

The window was open a little. He leaned over and stuck his nose out to get some air. Then he squeezed one eye shut and twisted his head around so he could see outside. With one hand he tried to open the window a little more, but it was stuck.

He took a deep breath and looked around with one eye. There was some snow on the lawns, and plenty up on the mountain, but the streets were bare. Elaine was piling snow up in a big lump and talking to herself.

Richard came into sight on his bicycle. He stopped when he saw Elaine. "Hey," he yelled, "have you seen Leroy?"

Elaine smashed a clump of snow on one side of her snowman. Then she stepped back to look at it. "Inside Mrs. Clausson's."

"What's he doing in there? You're crazy. He's probably down at the river."

Elaine put her mittened hands on her hips. "He's going to be a famous composer someday. Just like, uh . . . what's his name? Beet something?"

Richard started to laugh. "Now I know you're crazy. Leroy stinks at music. You ever hear him sing?"

Elaine stuck out her lip. "He is so taking piano lessons, Richard. And I can prove it."

"How?"

"We'll sneak right up and look in Mrs. Clausson's living-room window. That's where the piano is." She smacked a clump of snow on the other side of the snowman. "I guess you'll believe me when you see Leroy sitting right there, playing some . . ." She broke off. "Did you ever see a snowman with ears before? Looks pretty good, doesn't it?"

Richard lay his bike down on the road. "Okay, smarty," he said. "Let's just go take a look in Mrs. Clausson's window."

Leroy jerked his head in from the window. He looked in the mirror over the sink. There was a red ridge across the side of his cheek. He wondered how long he could stay in the bathroom? Until suppertime? Bedtime? Maybe he could make believe he had fainted. Fallen into the bathtub.

The doorknob rattled. Aunt Louise pounded on the door. "Leroy? Are you all right in there?"

He heard Mrs. Clausson calling down the hall. "What's the matter, Mrs. Everhart?"

Leroy looked at the tub again. He could dive right . . .

"I don't know what's keeping Leroy," Aunt Louise told her.

"Saints preserve us," Mrs. Clausson whispered as she came down the hall. "Sick last week . . . fainted? . . . bathtub . . . Call his mother."

Leroy took one last look at the tub, then opened the door.

"Oh," he said, looking surprised. "Are you looking for me?"

Aunt Louise was taking deep breaths. "I think I'd better sit down," she said.

"Don't you feel well, Aunt Louise? Maybe we should skip the piano lesson for today. I could come back some other . . ."

Aunt Louise took another breath. "I promised your mother," she said. "Go sit down at the piano. I'll be right with you."

Leroy walked back down the hall toward the living room. In back of him he heard Aunt Louise whisper to Mrs. Clausson, "Not like my Mitchell at all. I hope I live through this."

Leroy marched over to the piano. "It's awfully light in here," he told Mr. Twillig. "Don't you think we should pull the shades down!"

"Then I couldn't really see, now could I, Leroy?" Mr. Twillig said.

Leroy swallowed. Then he looked out the side windows. He didn't see Elaine or Richard. Maybe they

39

had changed their minds. He sat down at the piano and curled his fingers over the keys.

"Now," said Aunt Louise as she came back into the room. "I think we're ready to begin." She sat down heavily at the piano. "You'll be happy to know, Leroy, that I believe in starting right off with a piece of music. No scales in the beginning. Actual music."

Leroy shifted in his seat so he could get a good look in the mirror. He still couldn't see anyone outside.

Aunt Louise pulled a sheet of music off the top of the piano. "Here it is, Leroy. 'Singing Butterflies.' I'll play it for you the first time so you can hear how pretty it is."

With one hand Aunt Louise played: tum, tee, ta. Tum, tee, ta. Tum, tee, ta, tee, tum. At the same time, with her other hand, she fiddled with the large beads at her neck.

The piece sounded more like galloping elephants, Leroy thought, than singing butterflies. It was awful. A real baby thing.

Aunt Louise sat back and smiled at him. She seemed to be waiting for him to say something.

"What about the other hand?" he asked finally.

"Now we really can't expect to learn everything all at once," she said. "Our first piece is only for the right hand. You'll be able to learn this very quickly so that you can play at the recital with the rest of the children."

"Recital?"

"Certainly. I wouldn't want my pupils to work so hard and then have nobody hear them. I'm going to get a few more pupils, then hire a hall, and we'll send out invitations, and . . ."

Leroy pictured himself in a tuxedo in a concert hall. Everyone would be there. Richard in the front row, Tracy Matson next to him. He'd sit down at the piano on the stage. Everyone would be waiting. Then he'd play "Singing Butterflies" with one hand, and wave to the audience with the other.

It was too horrible to think about.

He looked into the mirror over the piano. Mr. Twillig had fallen asleep. As he checked out the window, he could see something move outside.

"Now Leroy," Aunt Louise said. "Put your fingers right here and play the C note. It's right in the middle. And then play D. Right next to the C."

Leroy moved his finger. There seemed to be about a thousand keys.

"Not the E note, Leroy. C."

Leroy looked down at the piano. The C note seemed to be right under the big *L* in the words *Lenox Piano*, which were written above the keys. Leroy stabbed at it, then looked up at the mirror.

"Very good," Aunt Louise said. "Now you see there are only a few notes in the whole piece. C, D, E. C, D, E. C, D, E, D, C. And you play that three times."

Leroy stared at the mirror. The pompom of Elaine's red hat appeared over the window ledge.

Leroy bent over in a fit of coughing. "I was sick last week, Aunt Louise," he said after he had kept it up for a few minutes. "I think my cold is coming back."

He slid off the piano bench and grabbed "Singing Butterflies" off the piano. "I'll practice this at home," he said, "but right now I'd better go to bed."

He nodded good-bye to Mr. Twillig, who had suddenly sat up straight. Without glancing at the window again, Leroy tore down the hall through Mrs. Clausson's kitchen and out the back door.

CHAPTER 6

Gideon Cole's cabin was halfway up Hubbell Mountain in a little clearing in the woods. Except for the bathroom, there was only one room. The stove and a cabinet were in one corner, and the bed in another. The rest of the room was a jumble of fishing lines, books, and other junk.

Gideon lived in the cabin all winter.

In the summer he went deep-sea fishing in a big boat out on the Atlantic Ocean. Then he'd come back in September and write books about his adventures.

Leroy was surprised every year when he didn't bring a wife back with him. Gideon must be almost thirty by now. But Gideon said he was waiting until he found someone who'd like to live up in the cabin all winter.

Leroy went up there every chance he could get.

It was Saturday again, a raw, gray day. Leroy thought about the roaring fire Gideon would have in the fireplace and the pile of hot corn bread in his oven.

Leroy shivered as he stood at the end of High Flats Road, watching everybody playing keep-away. Mitchell had grabbed the ball about five minutes ago and still hadn't passed it to anyone.

Leroy edged toward the mountain road. If the kids saw where he was going, they'd want to trail along too. Ordinarily he wouldn't have minded. But now everything was different.

Elaine would whine her way up the mountain, saying that it was too far and her feet hurt. And Mitchell would march into Gideon's cabin and take right over the way he had all week long.

Leroy waited until it looked as if everyone's back was turned, then he dashed across the dirt road and started up the mountain.

Behind him Elaine yelled, "Hey, Leroy, where are you going?"

Leroy hunched his shoulders and ran a little faster.

"Hey, Leroy," Elaine screeched.

He looked back over his shoulder. Mitchell was holding the ball under one arm. He looked up toward the mountain.

Leroy ducked behind a tree. He could hear Elaine yelling, "He is so up there. I saw him go up. What's he doing?"

Tracy said something, but Leroy couldn't hear what. He waited a minute, then peered arouna the edge of the tree. Mitchell had handed the ball to Tracy and was coming down High Flats Road toward the mountain.

Tracy and Elaine were right behind him.

Leroy darted to the next tree, then zigzagged behind a stack of slate that had been cut from the quarry.

Tracy was still at the bottom of the mountain. He could hear her yelling, "Come on, you guys, let's play."

But Mitchell had started up the mountain. "Don't worry," he yelled back to Tracy. "I'll spot him if he's up there. I'm good at that."

Leroy crawled around the side of the slate and looked down at Mitchell. A small stone next to his knee started to roll. Before Leroy could grab it, it skittered away from him and down the mountain.

"He's up there, all right," Mitchell shouted.

Leroy felt like picking up a rock and aiming for Mitchell's head. Instead he backed away from the slate. If Mitchell thought he could catch him on his own mountain, he was really crazy.

Leroy angled his way between two huge pine trees and headed for a small stream that splashed down from the top of the mountain. He ran along the muddy edge, trying to find a place to cross.

It took several minutes. He could hear Mitchell crashing through the trees behind him like an overgrown moose. Some wilderness guide he'd make, Leroy thought. There wouldn't even be an ant hanging around on the mountain if Mitchell didn't learn how to be a little quiet.

Finally Leroy spotted a large flat rock toward the opposite side of the stream. He looked at it, trying to decide if he could reach it in one jump.

He glanced over his shoulder. He could just about make out Mitchell's leather hat. Mitchell was really getting close.

Taking a deep breath, Leroy poised himself for the jump, and took a gigantic leap.

He landed right in the middle of the rock. He dug in with his sneakers, and stood there teetering for a second, before he hopped to the bank and scrambled up the side.

By this time Mitchell had reached the stream. "I've got you now, Leroy," he shouted. "You can't get away."

Leroy got to his feet and took off into the woods. Deliberately he moved away from the direction of Gideon's cabin.

Suddenly there was a splash. "Yeow," Mitchell screamed.

Leroy stopped running and looked back through the trees.

Mitchell was standing in the middle of the stream, water up to his knees, soaking wet. His leather hat and one leather glove floated away from him down the stream.

Leroy snapped an icicle off a low tree branch and sucked on it as Mitchell heaved himself up out of the stream, still on the opposite side. He watched Mitchell dance around, trying to wring out his clothes. His mother would probably kill him, Leroy thought, maybe keep him in the house for a week or two.

Served him right.

Still sucking on the icicle, Leroy turned and headed for Gideon's cabin. It took him about five minutes to get there, and for the last three he could smell something wonderful cooking.

It was Gideon's lunch.

46

Leroy knocked on the door and went inside.

Gideon was sitting at a wooden table in front of the fireplace. His plate was heaped with red beans.

He pointed to the stove with his knife. "Help yourself, Leroy," he said, his mouth full. "And take off those wet sneakers."

After Leroy stopped to pet Heidi, Gideon's German shepherd, he pulled off his sneakers and went over to the stove for some beans. He sat down at the table opposite Gideon. The warmth of the fire felt good on his back.

They ate without talking. Finally Gideon stood up and took a tray of muffins out of the oven. He slid two onto Leroy's plate.

"Well, Leroy," he said. "How's the bait business coming along?"

"We've been digging," Leroy said. "Trying to get ready." He thought guiltily that he still hadn't taken the worms out of Tracy's cellar.

Gideon looked out the window. "Won't be long now. It's getting cold. Going to snow again. Probably in a little while." He ambled over to the wall opposite the fireplace. About a dozen fishing poles hung there neatly in a row. Gideon touched them gently. "Take a look at this one, Leroy."

Leroy shoved the last of his muffin into his mouth and went over to the fishing rack. He looked at the jigging pole that Gideon had taken down. "Neat," he said.

"Old," Gideon said. "My first good one. Caught a twenty-four-inch pickerel under the ice with it."

Leroy nodded.

"I'm going to bring this down off the mountain next time I come to town. It's for you."

Leroy's mouth opened. "Why?"

Gideon grinned. "I thought about it this summer. I know you like to fish."

Leroy pictured himself on the frozen river. Tracy wouldn't be bragging that she had the best pole in High Flats anymore. And Mitchell. Mitchell would probably have some stinky-looking thing like Leroy's old one.

Leroy reached out to touch the pole. "Gee, Gideon . . ." he began. At the same moment, Heidi growled.

Leroy heard the clump of feet outside. Someone banged on the door.

As Gideon opened it, Mitchell staggered inside.

Leroy gritted his teeth.

Mitchell held out his hand to Gideon. "How do you do," he said politely. "I'm Mitchell Everhart, Leroy's cousin."

"Hello, I'm Gideon," Gideon said.

Leroy glared at Mitchell. The bottoms of Mitchell's pants were still wet. Little drops of water trailed after him on the floor.

It didn't seem to bother Mitchell one bit.

"I guess you'll be seeing a lot of me," he told Gideon.

"Well, that's good," Gideon said. "You look a little wet. I've got an extra pair . . ."

Mitchell waved his hand in the air. "Things like that

Mitchell held out his hand to Gideon.

don't bother me. Everyone in my other school said I was good at ignoring problems."

Leroy sat down at the wooden table again and rubbed Heidi's ears. If you listened to Mitchell often enough, he thought, you'd begin to think he was good at everything.

"How about something hot?" Gideon said.

Mitchell nodded. He sat down at the table next to Leroy and picked up a muffin. "Yes," he said. "I'm staying at Mrs. Clausson's for a while with my mother and sister. My father is, um . . . divorcing us."

Gideon pushed a plate of butter toward Mitchell. "You mean your father and mother are getting a divorce."

"I guess so," Mitchell said. "He said he's going to come see me when he gets settled somewhere."

Leroy tried to picture what it would be like not to have his own father around every day. For a minute he almost felt sorry for Mitchell.

But then Mitchell took a huge bite of his muffin. With a mouthful of crumbs, he told Gideon, "I'm going to start a guide business. I'll probably get Leroy to go in it with me. Take visitors around the mountain."

Leroy looked down at the table. He wished he could disappear.

Gideon cleared his throat. "We don't get too many visitors here, Mitchell. Outside of a few hunters in the fall and the ice fishermen . . ."

Mitchell smiled gently. "That's why I'm going to advertise." He slapped his hands on his knees. "But right now, Leroy, I think it's time for us to be heading down the mountain."

Leroy opened his mouth. Once and for all, he was going to . . .

Gideon looked out the window. "You know, he's right, Leroy. It looks to me as if it's going to start to snow any minute. In fact I think I see a few flakes right now. You wouldn't want to be stuck up here in a bad storm. With just me and the mountain monkeys to keep you company." Gideon shook his head and laughed.

"Mountain monkeys?" Mitchell.

"I'll leave that for Leroy to tell you. Right now you'd better get started," Gideon said.

Leroy sighed. He wondered if Gideon would want him coming up here anymore now that he had Mitchell hanging around, stuck to him like some kind of overgrown wart.

He said good-bye to Gideon. It was really starting to snow. He started down the dirt road ahead of Mitchell.

"Hey, wait up," Mitchell yelled.

Leroy turned. Every bit of what Mitchell had eaten in Gideon's cabin was smeared on his chin.

Mitchell caught up to him. "Nice guy, that Gideon," he said. "Let me know the next time you come up. I'll come too. Keep you company."

Mitchell babbled on about guiding visitors up to Gideon's cabin. Hardly paying attention, Leroy started to walk again. He kept thinking he'd never get to

Gideon's alone again. Never even walk on the mountain by himself. Unless . . .

He stopped dead, thinking about what Gideon had said. He wondered just how brave Mitchell was. Maybe he wasn't such a hero after all.

Leroy cleared his throat. "Mitchell, there's something I have to tell you."

Leroy looked back over his shoulder. He couldn't see Gideon's cabin anymore. And the snow was falling straight down, heavily. "Getting dark, isn't it?" he said to Mitchell.

Mitchell nodded.

"But maybe we could just sit down here for a minute?" He crawled under the branches of a tall evergreen and moved over to make room for Mitchell.

"You've heard of the Abominable Snowmen?"

"Of course," Mitchell said. "They're up on Mount Everest. I know all about them. Don't you remember I'm good at that scientific kind of stuff? The people who live there say that they're about five feet tall. Some of the mountain climbers have seen these huge footprints in the snow and—"

"They attack people," Leroy cut in. "Right?"

Mitchell looked serious. "They say so."

Leroy peered out from under an evergreen branch at the dark forest. "Listen, Mitchell. You heard what Gideon said."

"About the hunters?"

"Nah." Leroy lowered his voice. "About the mountain monkeys."

"I was going to ask you about—"

"Well, I'm going to tell you. Even though it's dangerous. We call the monkeys"—Leroy paused—"the Big Ones."

"What . . ."

"I wouldn't tell you this if you weren't my cousin . . ."

"And best friend," Mitchell added.

"Whenever someone tells on them," Leroy went on, "the monkeys come down off the mountains and kill that person too."

"Too?"

"They have long teeth . . ."

"Now wait a minute, Leroy," Mitchell broke in. "You don't think I'd really believe . . ."

Leroy crawled out from under the tree. "Forget it then. Why should I risk my life?"

"No, wait," Mitchell said.

Leroy turned around. "Do you think Gideon would have said anything about them if they weren't real?"

"But there aren't any monkeys up here in the north."

"Don't you understand?" Leroy said. "If the word got around that we had a monkey problem, do you think we'd have any hunters?"

Mitchell didn't answer.

"There's only one way to capture them," Leroy went on. "With a lasso. You have to keep yelling 'oh ha he ha' at the top of your lungs when you get near them."

Mitchell licked his lips. "Why would you do that?"

"It hypnotizes them or something. Then you have to whip out the rope, throw it around their necks, and say, 'I've got you.' "

"Then what happens?"

"They're supposed to drop dead. But who's going to try to capture one?" He looked up toward the top of the mountain. "Well, now I've told you. I guess they'll get me next."

Mitchell shook the snow off his shoulders. "It's really getting dark. Let's get out of here." He started to run.

"Wait a minute," Leroy yelled. "There's more. I still have to tell you the rest." He ran after him.

CHAPTER 7

At three o'clock on Monday afternoon, the bus doors shut, and Herbie the driver threw the bus into gear.

Leroy sat back and tried to figure out some things to be thankful for. Mrs. Claycomb had forgotten to collect the last couple of thankfuls and she had warned them at dismissal that she would collect them tomorrow.

Leroy glanced up at the front of the bus.

Elaine was sitting by herself, as usual, looking as if she was going to cry.

Mitchell was standing in the aisle explaining something to Tracy. As usual he was acting like a big shot with one finger up his nose.

Leroy nudged Richard. "I told him about the mountain monkeys," he said. "I said that the smell of city kids drove them crazy."

Richard started to laugh and slapped his knee. "Did you tell him they could smell a city kid for miles away and that sooner or later they'd come after him?"

Leroy nodded. "And eat his guts right out."

Richard pulled a candy bar out of his pocket. "Did

you remember about the worm? That's the best part."

"Sure. I said that the only way a city kid could save himself was to wear a dead worm around his neck. Even to bed. To get rid of the smell of being a city kid."

Richard stood up. "Wonder whether he's got one on?"

The bus pulled to a stop. "I don't know," Leroy said.

As the Windsor kids got off the bus, he pulled out a piece of paper. I AM THANKFUL, he wrote, TO HAVE A GOOD IMAGINASION.

A few minutes later it was his stop. Tracy and Mitchell got off ahead of him. Tracy was talking a mile a minute, making plans to set up guide signs all over the place.

"Well, I don't know," Leroy heard Mitchell say once. He noticed that Mitchell was looking up at Hubbell Mountain a little nervously.

Good. Leroy scraped a little snow off the ground to suck on, then circled around them and pounded down High Flats Road for home.

Fumbles was waiting for him, long tail wagging. Even his droopy eyes looked happy. Leroy dropped his books on the table, took Fumbles for a quick run outside, then came in and sat down at the piano.

He curled his fingers the way Aunt Louise had taught him, then crashed them down on the keys. They made a wonderful sound.

He pretended he was playing a great concert. The notes were loud and heavy.

"Not bad," he said to Fumbles, who was lying next to the piano bench looking at him with a blank expression. "But maybe you'd like something a little more simple. Something I used to play in my early days, before I became a famous piano player."

He stumbled through "Singing Butterflies." "You see, Fumbles, only three mistakes. I used to make six."

He went over to the television. "Enough practicing for today," he said. He switched it on and sat back to watch.

The phone rang right in the middle of a World War II movie on Channel 12. Guns were flashing, half the platoon had been killed, and the second lieutenant was wounded.

He picked up the phone. It was Tracy Matson.

"What do you want?"

"You'd better get over here, Leroy Wilson," Tracy said. "Right away."

"Can't," Leroy said. "Hang on." He ran over to the television, turned it up a little, and went back to the phone.

"Before my mother gets home, Leroy."

"Why?"

"Worms, that's why. They're all over the place."

Leroy sighed. "I meant to take them the other day," he said.

Tracy said, "Well, this is it, Leroy. Now."

Leroy heard her clunk the phone down, then he hung up and turned off the television. Pulling on his jacket, he rushed out the door.

Tracy had her front door open, waiting for him.

"You really did it this time, Leroy," she said. "You were supposed to take those worms off my hands weeks ago."

"How did they get loose?" Leroy followed her down the stairs to the cellar, blinking a little in the darkness.

"I can't remember everything," she answered, switching on the light. "I had to water them every day and . . ."

"Water?"

"I knew I'd have to teach you how to take care of them. Mr. Kirk said you had to water them with the watering can every day or they'd dry out." She pointed. "There they are," she said. "I mean, there they were."

In a corner was a wooden box, half covered by a screen. "I used an old windowscreen for the top," she said, "and took the bottom of the box apart and stuck a screen underneath too."

"It looks as if it's going to fall apart any minute," Leroy said. "No wonder . . ."

"Listen, Leroy. You've got to use screens. You pour water through the top and if it can't get out the bottom, they'll drown."

Leroy looked at the big puddle under the box. "Your mother . . ."

"Doesn't know one thing that's going on," Tracy said. "I threw all this junk in front of them." She pointed to a mound of old clothes and boxes that were lumped in the center of the floor. "I just pulled them apart for Mitchell."

"Mitchell?"

Tracy nodded. "He needed a worm. He's going to do

58

a special report on their habits. It's probably going to be published."

Leroy tried not to laugh.

"And you know what, Leroy?" Tracy went on. "That kid is really generous. He wanted to give me ten dollars for one stupid little worm. He said the ground was too frozen now to dig one up himself." Tracy shook her head. "But I didn't take it, of course."

"Of course," Leroy said, biting his lip. He looked around, trying to make himself think of something else before he had hysterics right there in front of her.

He stared down at the worm box. "I see a couple of worms."

"A couple," she said. "Are you crazy? We must have had seventy or eighty."

Leroy leaned over and wiggled his finger around in the dirt. "Maybe they're buried underneath somewhere."

"Don't even bother," Tracy said. "I know exactly where they are. Mr. Kirk told me."

"Where?"

"Well, he said they go for water every time. So I looked. He's right. They're in the laundry room." She shoved some clothes out of her way. "Maybe there are only eighty. But it seems like hundreds. All mixed up with the laundry."

She opened the laundry room door. "Step in carefully," she said.

Leroy leaned around the door. "I don't see any," he said.

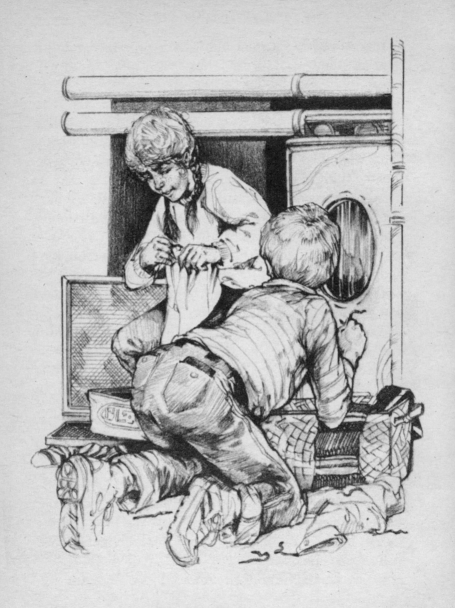

"You have to pick them off one by one," Tracy said.

Tracy crouched over a mound of clothes in a white plastic basket. "All the wet towels from the bathroom are in here," she said, "mixed in with the rest of the wash."

She held up an old yellow towel with strings hanging from the torn hem. About four worms were stretched across the towel. "See what I mean. You have to pick them off one by one."

Leroy sighed. By the time they straightened the whole mess out, the war would be over. He'd probably have to wait about a year until Channel 12 played it again. He knelt down next to Tracy.

She slid a can over next to him. "Just dump them in here for the time being. We'll put them in the box when we get finished." She glared at him. "And then you're taking the box home to your house. It's your turn."

"All right," Leroy said. "You don't have to get so excited. I was going to take them today anyway."

"Well, it's about time," she grumbled. "I've got another business going, you know."

"You mean wilderness guide?"

"Exactly."

"Listen, Tracy, you know as well as I do that there's no wilderness around here." He pulled a worm off a pair of Mr. Matson's work pants and dropped it gently into the can.

Tracy nodded reluctantly. "Well, maybe not wilderness exactly. But mountains, trees, stuff like that."

"You think anyone is going to ask you to guide them around a bunch of trees?"

She scooped two worms off the side of the laundry basket and nodded. "Yeah."

"Who?"

She thought for a minute. "Kids." She sat back on her heels. "I'll take them on nature walks." She narrowed her eyes. "That's really a terrific idea, if I do say so myself. I can't wait to tell Mitch. Except that he doesn't seem to be as excited about being a wilderness guide as he used to be . . ." She broke off. "Look at that fat one go."

Leroy picked up the worm. "That's the stupidest thing I ever heard of," he said.

"I bet Mitchell will think it's a terrific idea," Tracy said. "Just terrific."

"That's because Mitchell is a complete idiot."

Tracy stuck her finger in front of a worm that was trying to crawl up her sneaker. "Mitchell Everhart is a great guy," she said.

"He's an idiot."

"He is not. Just because he picks his nose once in a while. Everyone does that."

"And if you keep up this nonsense about being a wilderness guide," Leroy said, "everyone in the class will think you're a nut too. Hey." Leroy held up Mr. Matson's work shirt. "Look at all the worms on this. Maybe they like red plaid." He picked them off one by one. "Seven."

Leroy turned over the rest of the laundry, pulled a few more worms out of the bottom of the basket, and stood up.

"Wait a minute, Leroy," Tracy said. "Where are you going? I'll bet there are still a bunch of worms hanging around underneath something. That's the trouble with you. Always . . ."

Leroy didn't bother to answer. He stamped to the other side of the cellar and dumped the can of worms into the box.

"What about the rest of them?" Tracy said, her hands on her hips.

"I think we got them all," he said. "If not, you can bring them over later."

He put his arms around the box and heaved it up against his chest. He wondered if it would collapse before he could get it home. He maneuvered his way up the stairs, trying not to jostle it too much. Tiny clumps of dirt dropped through the screening in the bottom and plopped on the steps.

Behind him, Tracy climbed the stairs. "Everything always has to be your way," she said.

Leroy pushed open the side door with one shoulder and walked down her driveway.

"And another thing," she shouted after him. "You're jealous of your cousin Mitchell. Just because he's such a great guy."

Leroy turned back toward the door. "That's a rotten lie, Tracy Matson," he yelled. But it was too late. Tracy had slammed the storm door.

Shaking his head, he crossed her front lawn. Suddenly he wondered what time it was getting to be. Any minute his mother would be home from work.

And if she saw those worms, she'd probably make him dump them right back on the riverbank. He started to run as carefully as he could.

Five minutes later he was standing in the middle of his cellar. There was no place to hide the worms. At least no place that his mother or father wouldn't see as soon as they walked down the cellar stairs. He stood there for a minute looking around, then carried the worms back upstairs.

Outside, he could hear the sound of a car. He stopped to listen. It pulled into his driveway.

He dashed up the stairs, the box jouncing from one side to the other, dropping dirt, and opened the door to the attic. He just had time to slide the box onto the attic floor when he heard his mother calling him from the kitchen.

CHAPTER 8

It wasn't until a few mornings later that Leroy remembered the worms in the attic.

His father had left for work early that day and his mother had spent the whole breakfast time telling him that the great piano players practiced about seven hours at a time.

Leroy hadn't touched the piano in two days.

He wandered into the living room while his mother got ready to go to work in the factory in Windsor. He had about ten minutes until the school bus came. He twirled the piano stool around a couple of times, spread out his music, and sat down.

His mother's voice floated in from the hall. "If Mrs. Matson honks for me, Leroy, poke your head out and tell her I'm almost ready. I have to get something out of the attic."

Leroy sprang off the piano stool. "Don't do that," he yelled. He raced up the stairs after her.

"I thought you were practicing," his mother said and sighed.

"Don't worry. I have a slew of time right after school." He smiled at her. "I'll probably get in a couple of hours," he said, thinking that anyone who practiced "Singing Butterflies" with one hand for a couple of hours would probably be ready for the nut hatch. "What do you want up there anyway? I'll get it."

His mother smiled back. "If you think I believe you're going to practice 'Singing Butterflies' for a couple of hours . . ." She broke off and looked at him suspiciously. "I hope you haven't been up in the attic messing around with everything. I don't want . . ."

Leroy shook his head. "Why would I do that? Just tell me what you want."

"All right. My heavy blue coat. In the box next to the stairs. I think I'll need it today."

Leroy half-closed the door behind him and rushed up the stairs. Out of the corner of his eye, he glanced at the worm box, then he grabbed the coat and ran back down the stairs again.

There was no time to check on the worms before he had to leave for school. On the bus he wondered about them nervously. How could he have forgotten them? He hoped they were still alive. Even worms had to eat. He didn't even know what he was supposed to feed them. He hated to ask Tracy, but he could just imagine what she'd say if they starved to death.

As soon as he had taken off his coat and sat down at his desk, he tore a page out of his notebook and began to write:

Dear Tracy,
　　The grocery store is all out of the worm food I usually get. Since I have to buy something, I might as well get the same kind you've been using.
　　　　　　　　　　　　　　　　　　　Leroy

He folded the paper in half and waited for Mrs. Claycomb to bend over behind her desk. Leroy knew it would take her a minute to get up. Everyone knew she had a huge bag of candy in her bottom drawer. And even though she told them at least once a day that candy would rot their teeth away, she was always hiding behind the desk sucking on a piece of chicken corn or a chocolate candy kiss.

Now Mrs. Claycomb bent over. Quickly Leroy leaned across Richard and tossed the note onto Tracy's desk.

Tracy looked at the note, then over at him. Finally she took out her pencil. It was the great big fat yellow one that she was always bragging about.

It looked ridiculous.

Without opening the note, Tracy wrote something across the top and threw it back at him.

It whizzed across his desk and landed on the floor.

Leroy checked to make sure Mrs. Claycomb was still behind her desk, then bent down and picked up the note. Tracy had written:

I'M MAD AT YOU. KEEP THE WORM BISNIS. I'M GOING TO BE A WILDERNESS GIDE WITH MY FRIEND MITCH.

PATRICIA REILLY GIFF

Leroy looked over at Tracy, but she wasn't paying any attention to him. She had taken out a pencil sharpener and was sharpening her pencil.

In front of the room Mrs. Claycomb clapped for order. "First we'll do arithmetic, class. Then we're going to have a little reading test." She put about forty multiplication examples on the board, all with nines in them.

Usually, Leroy would have tried to be the first one finished. Math was his best subject after reading. And the nine times table was a snap.

But today he couldn't get started. Ever since Mitchell had come to High Flats, everything seemed to be going wrong.

By the time Leroy took out his looseleaf book, Mitchell had raised his hand and rushed up to the front of the room. "Excuse me, Mrs. Claycomb," Mitchell said.

Mrs. Claycomb looked up. "Yes, Mitchell, what is it?"

"I'm really good at nines," he said. "I know a terrific trick."

Wouldn't you know, Leroy thought.

Richard nudged him. "How does it feel to have a cousin who's a complete idiot?"

Leroy made a face. He wished Mitchell would just disappear. Vanish. Go back to New York City.

Leroy looked across at Tracy. She was staring at Mitchell as if he were Christopher Columbus and had just set foot in the New World.

Mitchell picked up a piece of chalk, examined it,

68

and exchanged it for a longer piece. "Maybe you'd like me to show the class, Mrs. Claycomb. It's really very simple. I taught everyone in my other school."

Mrs. Claycomb frowned. "I really don't think . . ."

"It will only take a minute," Mitchell broke in.

It was a good thing Mitchell was only ten, Leroy thought. Otherwise Mrs. Claycomb and her chicken corn would be right out of a job, and Mitchell and his terrific tricks right in.

Richard leaned over toward Leroy. "Do you think he's wearing his worm?" he whispered behind his hand.

Leroy grinned. "I hope so."

Mitchell blew on the chalk. "All the answers have to add up to nine," he said. He wrote "9 times 4" on the blackboard. "Can anyone tell me what the answer is?"

Richard looked at Leroy and made a face.

"Thirty-seven," Tracy shouted.

Mitchell cleared his throat again. "Almost," he said gently, a little smile on his face. "It's thirty-six."

Richard nudged Leroy. "Isn't that a string sticking out of Mitchell's T-shirt?" he whispered. "Is he wearing the worm?"

Leroy looked. But just then Mitchell moved. "I can't tell," Leroy said. He wondered what it would feel like to wear a dried-up worm. But if Mitchell was wearing one, it didn't seem to bother him at all. He kept talking about his dumb trick and how terrific it was if they could only get it.

The classroom door opened. It was the third-grade

teacher, Mrs. Weeks. She was Mrs. Claycomb's best friend. Mrs. Claycomb stood up and went out in the hall to talk with her.

Mitchell pointed to what he had written on the blackboard. "Look at the four. Take one less than four. Three, right? Now say three plus what is nine." He smiled. "Six. Right? You take the three and the six. Right?"

Leroy glanced at Tracy. Her mouth was open. She didn't understand one word her friend Mitch had said. Good.

Most of the other kids were talking now. The only one who was paying attention to what Mitchell was saying was Tracy.

Joe Bruno turned around in his seat. He looked at Leroy. "The kid looks just like you," he said. "It's amazing."

Leroy nodded reluctantly. "I guess so."

Joe shook his head. "I'd hate to have somebody like that look like me."

"If you think I like it," Leroy said, "you're crazy." He glanced up at Mitchell. Mitchell was still explaining his terrific trick. His voice was getting louder and louder. Every once in a while he looked at Tracy. "Right?" he asked. "Right?"

Tracy kept looking at her fat pencil.

Leroy began to copy the first example Mrs. Claycomb had put on the board: 421 times 93. It was hard to be sure which were Mrs. Claycomb's examples and which were Mitchell's.

Suddenly Tracy said, "Oh," in a loud voice. She

looked around the classroom. "Hey. That's right. It really works."

Mitchell beamed. "Yes. I told you . . ."

At that moment Mrs. Claycomb came back into the room. "There's too much noise in here," she said. She looked at the blackboard and frowned. "How are the children supposed to see which examples are mine?" she asked Mitchell. She took the eraser and erased Mitchell's work. "You may sit down now, Mitchell. I hope you get all of these right."

After Leroy did his arithmetic, he worked on the reading test that Mrs. Claycomb had handed out. He was the first one finished. Mary Redfern was second, and Mitchell third.

Tracy looked as if she would never finish her reading test. She kept moving her lips as she read each paragraph and making a terrible face. Every time she wrote an answer, she erased it again two seconds later.

Finally it was time to go home. It looked as if Tracy was still mad at him. She acted as if she didn't even see him when he climbed into the bus in back of her.

Leroy wondered what he was going to do about feeding the worms. They were probably waiting anxiously for something to eat. Or eating each other.

The bus ride seemed to take forever. Leroy sat there watching the gray slush piled up on the sides of the mountain road. When the bus finally stopped at High Flats, Leroy dashed out and raced up High Flats Road.

He didn't even stop to pet Fumbles at the front door. He went up to the attic and threw his jacket over an old chair.

The worms were still there, in the box in the corner. He dug around gently with his finger. They were moving around nicely and they didn't seem skinnier even though they hadn't eaten in a while.

Leroy sank down on the attic floor and tried to think about what to do. He wondered if he should take one of the worms down to the river and watch it to see what it ate. But he could see out the attic window that it had started to snow again. It really didn't seem like a good idea. Somehow he'd have to make up with Tracy. Right away. Before the worms starved to death.

CHAPTER 9

Leroy poked his head out of the kitchen door to see if it was snowing. The wind whistled around the side of the house and pulled at the door. It was freezing out. The temperature must have dropped a couple of degrees since he had gotten home from school an hour ago.

He banged out the side door, keeping his chin under his collar. Then he rushed down High Flats Road, looking for Tracy.

At the end of the road he stopped to read a sign that was flapping in the wind.

GUIDE SERVICE TO THE MOUNTAINS
SEE M. EVERHART OR T. MATSON
ON THE BRIDGE

Nuts. Both of them.

At least Mitchell knew how to spell *guide*. He looked up at the bridge. Tracy and Mitchell were standing there leaning against the rail.

"Hi, Leroy," Mitchell called. "Come on up."

"How many people are going to see that sign?" Leroy yelled up at them.

"A car went over the bridge just a few minutes ago," Mitchell answered.

"That's probably the first one in two days," Leroy said as he climbed up onto the bridge. He was glad to see that even Mitchell looked cold. He was all hunched up and kept stamping his feet up and down on the metal bridge.

Watching Tracy out of the corner of his eye, Leroy said, "The worms are coming along just fine."

Tracy didn't answer.

"I've been feeding them a special diet," Leroy went on a little louder. "It's supposed to make them double in size."

Mitchell nodded. "Too bad I couldn't have gone into business with you. I could have given you some advice. Helped out with the worms."

"But they don't seem to be very hungry," Leroy said. He edged over closer toward Tracy.

Tracy turned her back toward him and leaned over the side of the bridge to look down at the ice.

"I can't disappoint my customers though," Mitchell said, looking up at the mountain a little uneasily. "They're depending on me. You know what I mean?"

Customers nothing, Leroy thought. Mitchell was afraid to give up the guide business because of Tracy. Afraid he'd lose his only friend. Otherwise he'd never set foot on the mountain. Never go near those mountain monkeys.

74

Leroy pulled his hand out of his pocket and blew on his fingers. His nose was probably frostbitten. "Listen, Tracy," he said. "The worms are so used to the stuff you've been feeding them that they can't get used to the new food."

Tracy raised her shoulders a fraction of an inch. "We can go ice skating anytime now, Mitchell," she said. "Mr. Kirk drove his tractor across the river yesterday and cleared off the snow. He says the ice is plenty thick."

Leroy noticed she didn't look cold at all. Mitchell trailed behind her as she marched off the bridge and slid down the path Mr. Kirk had made with his tractor.

"Thick as a turnip," Tracy yelled up. She began to take gliding steps. "I think I'm going to be an Olympic ice skater when I grow up."

Leroy stood there shivering as Mitchell took a flying leap onto the ice. "Maybe I could practice with you," Mitchell said to her. "I'm good at sports."

Leroy pictured the worms in the attic, getting skinnier by the minute. "Hey, Tracy . . ." he began.

Behind him there was a clanking noise. It was Elaine. She was coming down High Flats' Road wearing a pair of brand-new ice skates. He could tell she had never worn skates before. She was practically walking on her ankles.

When she got to the top of the riverbank, she stopped. "I can't get down there with these skates on, Mitchell," she yelled. "It's too steep."

Leroy shook his head. He didn't know which one

75

was worse: Mitchell sliding around on the ice like some kind of a windmill or crybaby Elaine.

Elaine cupped her orange mittens around her mouth. "Mitchell," she screeched. "You have to help me."

"Get lost," he shouted.

Elaine sat down on the top of the bank and started to inch her way down. "I'm going to fall, Mitchell," she screamed.

Mitchell pulled his hat down farther over his eyes. "Do you have to follow me all over the place?" he yelled. "You can't skate anyway."

"I'm going to tell Mother," she said, beginning to cry. "You'll be sorry."

Mitchell took a couple of running steps in the other direction, then slid along the ice for about three feet.

"Hey, Mitch," Tracy yelled. "That was great. Really terrific."

"I'm going to tell everybody what . . ." Elaine began.

Mitchell stopped gliding on the ice. He took a step toward her.

"Don't you dare touch me, Mitchell Everhart," she yelled. She scrambled up the riverbank and clanked away down High Flats Road.

"What's the matter with her?" Tracy asked as she slid back toward the bridge.

Mitchell shrugged. "All she does is cry."

Leroy felt his nose tingling. The rest of his face was tingling too. Any minute he would fall off the bridge. He'd be stiff before he hit the ice. Frozen to death. And all because of a bunch of worms.

"Don't you dare touch me, Mitchell Everhart."

"This is your last chance, Tracy," he yelled. "I'm going into the house to get warm."

"You'd better tell him, Tracy," said Mitchell. "It isn't good for business to sell worms that don't have proper nourishment."

Tracy put her hands on her hips. She looked up at Leroy.

"Admit it, Leroy."

"What?"

"You've been starving those poor worms up at your house."

"I have not."

"You don't know what to feed them."

"I do so," he shouted. "I've been giving them a special blend of . . ."

Tracy giggled. "Manure, Leroy. Right out of Mr. Kirk's barn. And not a special blend either. Anything you can get your hands on." She made a face. "Or shovel on, I should say."

Leroy stepped back. "You don't mean . . ."

Tracy slid along the ice until she was directly under the bridge. "Poop," she shouted up. "Chicken poop. Or rabbit poop."

"Argh," Leroy said. He curled his lips back over his teeth, picturing himself carrying piles of manure up to his attic. He stared at Tracy, not sure whether he should believe her.

"Whew," Mitchell said. "I'm glad I'm not in the worm business. I guess it's easier to be a guide." He and Tracy looked at each other and laughed.

Leroy grit his teeth. Mitchell was ruining his whole

life. Acting like an idiot in school when everyone knew they were cousins. Taking Tracy away.

"Hey," Mitchell yelled. "Here comes another car. See, Leroy, business is picking up."

"That's no customer," Tracy said, looking up the mountain road. "It's only Gideon coming down in his Jeep." She started to slide away. "Come on, Mitchell. Let's go around the bend."

Leroy waited for the Jeep to cross the bridge.

"Hi," he called as Gideon pulled to a stop next to him and opened the door. Suddenly he wondered about Mitchell. He hoped Mitchell hadn't said anything about the mountain monkeys or wearing a worm around his neck.

"Pretty cold out there," Gideon said. "Is that Tracy and Mitchell down on the ice?"

Leroy nodded.

"How's Mitchell settling in? All right?"

"I guess so," Leroy said uneasily.

"Good," Gideon said. "I figured you'd get him all set up. Introduce him around. Make sure he felt comfortable. It's pretty hard to move to a new place."

Leroy nodded again, thinking that it probably wasn't hard at all for Mitchell to move to a new place. Mitchell just moved right in and took over.

Gideon reached into the back of the Jeep. "I brought down the jigging pole for you. Figured the ice would be pretty thick by now. It's about time for some ice fishing." He handed the rod to Leroy. It was packed in a gray flannel case.

"Wow," Leroy said, rubbing his hand along the soft

flannel. "Thanks a lot, Gideon. It's the best one in High Flats."

"Hope your bait business is ready," Gideon said. "I have some friends. About eight of them. They're coming weekend after next to do some ice fishing. They're going to stay at Mrs. Clausson's boardinghouse."

"I'll be ready."

"Good." Gideon glanced down at the ice where Tracy and Mitchell were sliding back into sight. "Nice for you to have Mitchell here now. I guess he's a new partner in the worm business."

Leroy opened his mouth and looked at Gideon. He wanted to say that Mitchell was an idiot and he'd rather give up the whole business than be stuck with Mitchell as a partner. But Gideon would never understand.

"Yes," Leroy heard himself say, "Mitchell's a partner, all right. He certainly is."

CHAPTER 10

Leroy sat up in bed the next morning and looked out the window. It was snowing so hard he could hardly see the houses on the other side of High Flats Road.

He got up and stepped over Fumbles, who was curled up asleep next to the bed. Gideon's jigging rod lay across the dresser. Leroy picked it up and sat down on the bed again.

Then he remembered what he had said to Gideon yesterday. About Mitchell being his partner.

How could he have been so dumb? Now he'd have to ask Mitchell to join the worm business.

That creep.

He pulled gently on the little spring at the end of the jigging pole. Maybe Mitchell would say no. Maybe Mitchell would say he was too busy in the guide business.

Not a chance. Not Mitchell. He'd be right there ready to ruin everything.

Leroy could hear his mother rattling around downstairs. He got up, threw on some jeans, and went down to the kitchen.

"What about school?" he asked. "It's snowing pretty hard."

His mother handed him a glass of orange juice. "You're in luck," she said. "We've got about eight inches of snow and more coming. I just heard it on the radio. No school."

Leroy grinned. He took a swallow of juice. He was always thirsty in the mornings. "Are you going to work?" he asked.

"Have to, Leroy. The plow's out."

Leroy tried to look sympathetic. "Too bad," he said, thinking that it was terrific. If his mother was home, she'd be all over the place, telling him to straighten his room, do some extra-credit reports, or stumbling over the worms up in the attic. "Maybe you'd better leave early," he told her.

"I'm going to." She took a gulp of coffee and went upstairs to get ready.

"Don't forget, you have a piano lesson at four o'clock this afternoon," she called over her shoulder.

Leroy banged his juice glass down on the table. There was always something to ruin things.

Then he sat down at the table and started to eat his cereal while he waited for his mother to leave for work.

As soon as she was gone, he lifted the bowl to his mouth and slurped down the last few drops. Then he filled the teakettle and went up to the attic.

Before he began to water the worms, he pulled one of his mother's summer curtains out of a carton and spread it around next to the box. Every day it seemed a little more water seeped through the screen in the bottom, and if it ever went through the attic floor, he'd be in enough trouble to last all winter.

Squatting down on the floor, he dribbled the water carefully into the box, making sure he didn't hit any of the worms.

He sniffed. The attic was beginning to smell a little from the rabbit manure he had been sneaking upstairs the last few days.

He went over to the window. There were about a million dead flies on the sill left over from last summer. He blew some of them off and pried the window up an inch.

High Flats Road looked wonderful, all white under the swirling snow.

Too bad he really couldn't enjoy it. And all because of Mitchell. He thought about what Gideon had said. About settling in. He'd like to settle Mitchell right in. With a bulldozer.

If only the Everharts weren't here, he wouldn't have to worry about playing "Singing Butterflies" in a piano recital. In front of the whole world.

And even his fight with Tracy was all because of Mitchell.

He pictured himself inviting Mitchell to be in his business. He thought about being stuck with Mitchell and his messy mouth down at the river on weekends for the rest of the winter.

Maybe he'd wait. At least until after lunch. He'd do

some shoveling as soon as it stopped snowing a little. Tracy always did her own and Mrs. Schaeffer's walk, but he did all the rest.

He'd make a pile of money.

He went downstairs and played "Singing Butterflies" three times as fast as he could. Then he turned on the TV and stretched out on the couch.

Fumbles came into the living room and lay down on the rug.

Leroy patted the cushion at one end of the couch. "It's too snowy to go out yet," he said. "Come on up here."

Fumbles rolled his eyes. He knew he wasn't supposed to get up on the furniture.

Leroy patted the couch a little harder. "Don't worry," he said. "We have the whole day to do what we please. Think of it as a vacation."

Reluctantly Fumbles climbed onto the couch. He settled himself at one end and sighed.

Leroy sighed too. He just couldn't seem to concentrate on *Name That Number*. He kept thinking about the piano recital, and Mitchell. He began to wonder about yesterday's reading test. He usually got the highest mark in the class, and Tracy Matson usually got the lowest.

Finally he got up off the couch and looked out the window. It was still snowing, but much less than before. He figured he'd get his shovel out and go down to Mrs. Clausson's. Before he shoveled her walk, he'd ask her if he could put a little sign up on her bulletin board in the dining room.

He rummaged around in the kitchen for a pad and a pencil, then he wrote in large block letters:

RED WORMS FOR SALE
BIG AND LIVELY
GREAT FOR CATCHING PERCH AND PICKEREL
SEE LEROY WILSON
BROWN HOUSE ON HIGH FLATS ROAD
OR AT THE RIVER

He put the sign in a paper bag so it wouldn't get snow all over it, then went into the storeroom and tugged on his boots.

Outside, the snow had almost stopped. He took the snow shovel out of the garage and trudged down High Flats Road.

At Mrs. Clausson's he banged his boots against the stone step, thinking that his feet hurt already, and went inside.

Mrs. Clausson was in the kitchen, making biscuits. At the table next to her Elaine was dropping raisins into the dough.

"Nice to have a day off," Mrs. Clausson said.

"I'm making biscuits," Elaine said.

Leroy nodded at both of them and took the sign out of the bag. "Can I hang this in the dining room?"

Mrs. Clausson dried her hands on a towel. "I'll do it for you."

"Thanks," Leroy said. "I guess I'll get to your shoveling now. All right?"

Mrs. Clausson looked a little upset. "I'm sorry, Leroy.

Mitchell asked me about that before. He was up early. About seven. He asked me first."

Leroy swallowed. "Mitchell?"

In back of him Mitchell banged into the kitchen dropping clumps of snow all over the floor. He clapped his snowy gloves together. "Glad you're finally up, Leroy," he said. "How would you like to go into business with me?"

"And be a guide? I told you . . ."

Mitchell shook his head. "No, I can handle that by myself. It's this snow-shoveling business. I have . . . let me see . . . Mrs. Clausson, Mrs. Grant, Mrs. Schaeffer . . . I guess just about everybody in High Flats. And I promised them all I'd have their walks shoveled before noon."

"Why don't you boys go outside?" Mrs. Clausson said, bustling around between the two of them. "I've got to finish up in here and start the beds. And I can't get anything done with you here."

Mitchell jerked his head toward the door. "Yeah, come on, Leroy. Let's go outside. Decide how we're going to divide this whole thing up. Get started. Get finished. That's what I always say."

Leroy could feel his face getting red. There was a fist-sized lump in his chest. He turned and walked out of the kitchen behind Mitchell.

Outside, the snow was blowing around, making it hard to see. He stood on Mrs. Clausson's back step, his hands clenched at his sides. When he spoke, he was so angry it was hard to make his mouth move the way he wanted it to and his voice felt hoarse.

"Listen, Mitchell, I've had enough of you."

"Listen, Mitchell," he said. "I've had enough of you. You've messed up everything since you got here." He blinked furiously, not sure if the snow was getting into his eyes or whether he was actually crying.

Mitchell opened his mouth. "What are you talking about?" he asked, then leaned closer to Leroy. "Are you crying?"

"That's just the kind of idiotic thing you'd say. It's the snow." He rubbed his eyes with the back of his hand.

"What's the matter with you anyway?"

"You don't even know, do you? Well, who do you think has been shoveling snow around here before you came?"

Mitchell opened his mouth again.

"Me," Leroy shouted. "Me."

He pushed past Mitchell and rushed out of Mrs. Clausson's yard. He stopped at the driveway and yelled back, "If it wasn't for you and your mother and your sister, I'd have some peace around here. I wouldn't have to worry about a bunch of lousy singing butter-flies and practicing the piano every two minutes and making an idiot of myself at a recital in front of the whole lousy world."

He ran up High Flats Road for home, not bothering to wipe his tears away. He didn't even stop when he saw Tracy Matson at her living-room window tapping on the glass to get his attention. He pulled open his back door and went into his kitchen, thinking that he'd rather die than ask Mitchell to be a partner in his worm business.

CHAPTER 11

It was three minutes before four. Leroy had spent most of the afternoon lying on the living-room couch with Fumbles, watching television. He sat up and tried to decide if he should go to the piano lesson or call his mother at work and tell her he thought he had a cold again.

She'd never believe it.

He stood up and went over to the window. Mitchell was down at the end of the road, still shoveling snow. He had been at it all day. He had shoveled the whole town of High Flats. Single-handed. He probably had blisters all over himself.

Good.

He stared at Mitchell. Mitchell would probably tell everybody in the whole school that Leroy had been crying. Over a snow-shoveling job. They'd think he was a big baby. And so would Tracy Matson. He wondered if Mitchell had told her yet.

Every time he thought about it he got madder.

He picked up his music from the top of the piano, stopped at the storeroom for his jacket, then went out the back door. He trudged down the driveway and peered around the corner of the house.

Mitchell was still there. He was standing in the middle of Mrs. Schaeffer's walk, leaning on his shovel.

Leroy hated to walk past him. He didn't even want to look at him. And he didn't want Mitchell yelling stuff at him about being a baby either.

Slowly he started down High Flats Road. Across the street Tracy was sitting at her front window again. She banged on it and motioned to Leroy.

Suddenly he realized that Tracy had been in the house all day. He wondered if she was sick. Or maybe she was mad at Mitchell too.

He stopped short. Mitchell was shoveling Mrs. Schaeffer's walk. That was Tracy's job.

He nodded to himself. Maybe now Tracy would realize that Mitchell wasn't so hot after all.

Leroy crossed the street. By this time Tracy was standing at her front door. She poked her head out. "Hey, Leroy," she yelled. "Come on over."

He went up the path, kicking the snow in front of him.

Tracy put her head out a little farther. She took a deep breath. "It's stuffy in here. Smells wonderful out-doors."

"What are you doing in the house then?" he asked. "And how come Mitchell's doing Mrs. Schaeffer's walk?"

"I can't come out." She bent over and made a snow-ball out of the snow that was lying on the doorsill.

"Are you sick?"

"Sick of school. I failed that test. Mrs. Claycomb called last night. My mother said I had to stay in all day and study. She's mad as a rattlesnake in August." She jerked her head toward Mitchell. "I told you he was a nice guy. Not many kids would do what he did."

"What?"

"He came over early. When he found out about my being stuck in here all day with nothing to do, he said he'd do everybody's walk with you and cut me in for a third."

She tossed the snowball at him. "I really need the money anyway. My jigging pole stinks."

Leroy stood still. He didn't know what to say. "What made Mitchell think I'd do the walks with him? Who told him to organize this whole thing?"

"Just the goodness of his heart, I guess."

Leroy heard the sound of Mitchell's shovel scraping against Mrs. Schaeffer's front walk. He glanced toward him. Mitchell was shoveling again. As fast as he could. Leroy could see the snow flying up in the air behind him and settling in clumps on the side of the path.

Tracy leaned out a little farther and scraped a big *T* with her foot on her snowy step. She was saying something about the worms. Leroy looked back at her. "What?"

"I said, I'm back in the worm business. B-A-C-K," she yelled.

Leroy thought for a minute. Tracy had really done most of the work. "Okay," he said, and looked up. "Why?"

"I don't have any money. Not one cent. Even with

the snow money I still don't have much. And after all, I practically raised those worms."

"I said all right."

"I hope you're taking care of them."

Leroy nodded, watching Mitchell out of the corner of his eye.

"Did you get plenty of Mr. Kirk's manure?"

Leroy nodded again. Mitchell was probably trying to show him how hard he was working. Waiting for Leroy to apologize. Well, he'd have a long wait. That idiot.

"Water them?"

"Huh? Listen, Tracy. I don't have time to hang around and talk about worms. My piano lesson should be half over by now."

He backed down the path toward High Flats Road.

This morning the plow had left a huge bank of snow on each side of the road. He climbed up on it and maneuvered his way down the street toward Mrs. Clausson's. Halfway there, snow caved in under him and he sank into it to his knees. It was freezing.

He scrambled up, trying to keep his music dry. Behind him the sound of the shovel had stopped. Leroy glanced over his shoulder. Mitchell was standing at the end of Mrs. Schaeffer's path, watching him.

"Hey, Leroy," he called. "Wait up. Where are you going?"

Leroy didn't answer. He jumped off the snowbank and headed up Mrs. Clausson's front walk.

Aunt Louise was waiting for him at the door. She opened it wide. Today she was wearing an orange striped dress with a long necklace of yellow beads. They clicked when she moved.

"Look at you," she said. "You're going to catch your death of cold one of these days. Covered with snow." She stood back to let him pass her, then poked her head out the door.

"Don't get wet, Mitchell," she called.

She turned back to Leroy. "Let's get down to some music."

Leroy followed her into Mrs. Clausson's living room. He slid onto the piano bench, nodding at Mr. Twillig, who was sitting in his chair carving a small piece of wood with his penknife.

"Well," said Aunt Louise. "I have quite a surprise for you, Leroy, as soon as you play 'Singing Butter-flies.'"

Leroy poised his fingers over the keys for a second, then swooped down and raced through "Singing Butterflies."

As he played the last note, Aunt Louise sighed. "Try it once more, Leroy," she said. "This time play it a little slower."

Leroy pretended he was playing for a funeral. Mitchell's. He played one note after the other as slowly as he could.

Aunt Louise sighed again. "That sounds more like a funeral," she said. "But never mind." She stood up and paged through a pile of music on the top of the piano. Then she pulled out a piece. "'Drums,'" she said, beaming. "'Drums in the West.' You're going to love it."

Leroy looked at her with interest. Anything would be better than "Singing Butterflies."

"If you really work at this, you'll be able to play it for the recital." She spread the music out.

It had lots of black notes. Much better, Leroy thought.

Aunt Louise played it once for him. Then she listened to him as he fumbled through it.

"Much better, right?" Aunt Louise said. "Mitchell said so."

"Mitchell?"

"Yes. He told me this morning that it was ridiculous for a boy to play 'Singing Butterflies.' " She frowned. "Lousy butterflies, he called them. Now I really don't agree. Anyone can appreciate a butterfly. But since it's your first recital, I'll let you play 'Drums.' It was Mitchell's second piece too." She wagged her finger at him. "But I warn you. The recital is next Friday night. You'll have to work hard."

"Friday?"

She smiled. "Yes. I was able to persuade Reverend Adams to lend us the church hall. I'm going to send out invitations."

Leroy's heart sank. "I can't . . . it's too . . ."

Mrs. Clausson appeared at the living-room door. "I'm sorry to interrupt," she told Aunt Louise, "but Mrs. Wilson is on the phone. She wants to talk to you."

"One minute," Aunt Louise said. "We're just about finished here anyway." She turned to Leroy. "Practice hard," she said. "We'll have a few little lessons next week to be sure you're ready." She patted him on the shoulder. "Don't worry though, if you can't get it ready by then. You can always play 'Singing Butterflies.'" She stood up and swept out of the room.

Leroy slid off the piano bench and nodded to Mr. Twillig. But Mr. Twillig was sound asleep, his mouth open. Leroy tiptoed out of the living room and went into the hall to put on his boots.

By the time he got outside, it was getting dark. Mitchell was nowhere in sight.

Mitchell. Suddenly he remembered that Mitchell had gotten him out of playing "Singing Butterflies." That Mitchell had to stick his big nose into everything. And even though this new piece was about a thousand times better than "Singing Butterflies," it wasn't going to make him like Mitchell one bit more.

CHAPTER 12

In the kitchen Leroy's mother was setting the table with the best plates. She smiled at him. "How was the piano lesson?"

"The recital is next Friday."

"Good."

"Stinks," Leroy said.

"You'll be fine."

"Listen, Ma, you don't really expect me to get up there in front of the whole world and look like a complete idiot. Do you?"

His mother put the salt and pepper on the table. "I've been listening to you, Leroy. You sound better every day."

Leroy groaned. "Hey," he said, suddenly noticing the plates on the table. "What are all these for?"

"Aunt Louise, Mitchell, and Elaine. Dad has to work late so I called and invited them for dinner."

Leroy slammed his rolled-up music on the counter. "I am sick of them," he said slowly and distinctly. "*Sick of* . . ."

"You don't mean that. Anyway, not now. They'll

probably be here any minute. Put your music away like a good boy and finish setting the table." She went over to the stove and stirred a pot of string beans. "There's the door now."

Leroy went into the living room and laid the music on the piano. He could hear Aunt Louise in the hallway. She was stamping her feet to get the snow off them and talking to his mother. "Lovely of you to have us for dinner, Karen."

"Just hamburgers," his mother said. "Leroy," she called. "Mitchell and everybody are here."

Leroy banged his fist on top of his music. He could tell by his mother's voice that she expected him to come running. She wanted him to act as if the Queen of England were here with the prince and princess.

He stamped into the hall. "Umpf," he said to Mitchell, and followed the rest of them into the kitchen.

He gave Fumbles a pat and slid into his seat. Mitchell stood there holding Leroy's mother's chair.

"Sit down, Aunt Karen," he said and pulled out the chair for her.

"What a little gentleman," she said as Mitchell went back to his seat next to Leroy.

For a moment there was silence. Everyone was passing hamburgers, string beans, French fries, and tomatoes around. Leroy glanced at Mitchell.

The little gentleman had ketchup all over his plate, the tablecloth, and his face.

And his mouth was open. Wide. You could see about a ton of hamburger being ground into mush.

The little gentleman had ketchup all over his face.

Horrible.

Mitchell caught him staring and clapped him on the back. "Feeling better now?" Mitchell asked under his breath.

Leroy twitched his back away from Mitchell.

Leroy's mother stopped spooning tomatoes onto her plate and looked at Leroy carefully. "Better?" she asked. "Your throat again?"

"Leroy was just a little out of sorts today," Mitchell said.

Leroy shot him a look of pure hatred. "Nothing's the matter."

Across from him Elaine was whispering to her mother in a voice that Gideon could probably hear halfway up the mountain. "What are those little things in the hamburgers? They taste awful."

"Hush," Aunt Louise said.

"*I hate them*," Elaine whispered.

"Onions," Leroy's mother said. "They're just onions. But I could get you something else instead. Maybe some soup or . . ."

"My children like all kinds of food," Aunt Louise answered, glaring at Elaine. "Let's talk about the recital. So exciting."

"It certainly is," said Leroy's mother.

Leroy speared a string bean. He noticed that Elaine was dropping her hamburger by the handful to Fumbles under the table.

"I hope Leroy has a suit," Aunt Louise said.

"Well," said his mother a little doubtfully. "There's

that one from last year." She frowned a little. "Why did we buy that suit anyway?"

Leroy swallowed. "Fiftieth anniversary of the church. But I'm not going to . . ."

"Yes," his mother said. "But actually that was about a year and a half ago. In the summertime. I hope that suit still fits."

"Probably won't," Leroy said. "But look, Aunt Louise, I'm going to skip . . ."

"Oh no," said his mother firmly. "We'll get you into it somehow."

"I'm sure you'll manage something, Karen," Aunt Louise said. "I'm going to send handwritten invitations to everyone in High Flats: the minister, the teachers, Mrs. Bemus, the principal"—she waved her hands around—"everybody." She paused. "Mitchell has a lovely brown jacket. Corduroy. With a velvet collar."

Leroy glanced at Mitchell. Mitchell looked a little uncomfortable. Maybe he didn't like his lovely brown jacket. Leroy grinned to himself. Or maybe the worm he had around his neck felt all scratchy.

"I'm going to wear a pink dress, Leroy," Elaine said. "It's long to the floor. With lace. You're going to like it, I bet." She smirked at him and handed Fumbles another hunk of hamburger.

"Don't do that," Aunt Louise said. "Eat nicely." She turned to Leroy. "I meant to tell you this afternoon. I met a friend of yours last night. He stopped in at Mrs. Clausson's to say hello to Mr. Twillig."

Leroy looked up at her.

"I forget his name. Grover? Or was it Gary?"

"Gideon?" his mother suggested.

"Yes, Gideon. He said we're going to have some ice fishermen here next weekend."

"Yes," Leroy's mother said. "It's the season."

"Gideon told me that Leroy and Mitchell, and that girl . . . the one with braids . . ."

"Tracy Matson?"

"Yes, Tracy Matson . . . were in business together." Aunt Louise made a face. "He said they're going to sell worms."

Everyone started to speak at once.

"Is Tracy Matson keeping worms in her . . ." his mother began.

"Gee, I don't know, Leroy," Mitchell was saying. "I'm pretty tied up in the guide . . ."

"Such a messy thing to get involved in . . ." Aunt Louise said.

And over everyone else, Elaine was screaming, "*I want to be in it too. Why can't I be in it? Mitchell never lets me do anything. I want . . .*"

"Be quiet," Mitchell shouted at her. "You can't be in it. We've done all the work. I'm quitting if Elaine has to be in this."

Aunt Louise looked at the ceiling. "Give me patience," she said. "I'm sure Elaine can have a little part in it. Maybe she could just carry a pail of worms or . . ."

"*Wait a darn minute,*" Leroy yelled.

"Simmer down a little," his mother said, putting her

hands over her ears. "I know it's exciting for you to be in business together, but you are bursting my eardrums."

Leroy stuffed a tomato in his mouth. He couldn't believe what was happening. "Listen," he said, as soon as he could talk.

"I always felt bad for you," his mother went on, "when winter came and Richard couldn't get across the mountain. Well, I'm going to add a little something to this wonderful news. I got some overtime money in my paycheck today. And I'm going to buy you a pair of work boots. Just like Mitchell's."

Leroy didn't answer. He'd rather stuff his feet in his old boots for the next ten years than take Mitchell into the worm business. But then he thought about Gideon. What would Gideon think if he knew that?

And what would Gideon think if he ever found out Leroy had told Mitchell that there really were mountain monkeys? Or that stuff about wearing dead worms. Gideon would never understand.

"Leroy?" his mother asked. "I thought you'd be thrilled. You've been asking for . . ."

"I am," Leroy said. "I really am. I've been wanting work boots for a long time. But . . ."

"Good," said his mother. "Have another hamburger."

As she passed the platter, Mitchell leaned over toward him. "I'm going to give you a third of that shoveling money," he whispered.

Leroy shook his head. "Keep your darn money."

"What money?" Elaine asked.

"Shut up," Mitchell said.

Leroy took a bite out of his hamburger.

"On second thought," Mitchell whispered when Aunt Louise began to talk again, "I've got to give up the guide business." He paused and went on in a lower voice. "Because of the mountain monkeys. The Big Ones. After all, my mother and sister need me now that my father is . . ." He broke off and began again. "So I can spend a lot of time working on the bait with you." He dumped some ketchup on his last bite of hamburger. "Yes, you're right. I'll hold on to the money for a while. Maybe pour it into the business when things get going."

"Well, everybody," Leroy's mother said, "I've got one more surprise. Butter pecan ice cream with chocolate syrup and whipped cream for dessert."

Leroy stood up. "I'm going outside. To take Fumbles for a walk."

Mitchell started to get up.

Leroy glared at him. "I'll be back," he said. "Stay right there."

CHAPTER 13

On Friday night, a week later, Leroy climbed the stairs to his bedroom. He had about a half hour to get ready for the recital.

He picked up his red tie and held it to the light. There was a little spot of gravy in the center, left over from the fiftieth anniversary party, but his mother had told him that once he tucked it under his jacket, no one would notice.

He sat down on the edge of the bed. It had been a terrible week. Terrible.

The day after the hamburger dinner, Mitchell had changed the sign in Mrs. Clausson's dining room. Now it said L.M. and T. BAIT SERVICE on the top.

And Mitchell kept asking him so often how the worms were coming along that it began to sound as if Mitchell were their father and Leroy the wicked stepmother.

On Tuesday, when he had asked Leroy for the fourth time if they had been watered enough, Leroy stuck his head up next to Mitchell. "If you say one more word about these worms," Leroy said, "I'm going to throw them right down the toilet bowl and that will be the end of the whole L.M. and T. Bait Service. It may even be the end of you."

After that, Mitchell was a little better. But not much. He spent most of the time talking to Tracy. Once Leroy heard him say that he was drawing up plans to build a bait store that would sit right on top of the ice. He was so excited that he was jumping all over the place.

Tracy had looked a little doubtful. "It would sink in the river at the first thaw," she said. "Don't you think that would be a lot of work for nothing? We could just as easily put it on the shore next to the river. Use it for something during the summer too."

Tracy and Mitchell had spent the rest of the week working on the plans. Tracy borrowed a rug from Mrs. Grant, and Mitchell ran all over the place looking for roofing tiles and windowpanes.

The whole thing was ridiculous.

But that wasn't the worst. The worst was Aunt Louise's plans for the recital. She had sent handwritten invitations to everyone in the whole world, it seemed. Mrs. Claycomb was coming, and everyone in High Flats.

And on the bus coming home from school today, Richard told him that his mother and father were bringing him too.

Leroy had stared at Richard in horror. Richard still didn't know that he was taking piano lessons. He spent most of the ride home trying to talk Richard out of coming, but Richard said that it would probably be as good as a circus. Mitchell was not only playing the piano, but he was doing a violin solo too. And Elaine was going to sing a song straight out of opera and accompany herself on the piano.

Richard slapped his knee and nudged Leroy. "Can't you just see it, Leroy?" he asked. "That pair of idiots. I'm going to be right there. Sitting in the front row." He grinned. "Wonder who else is going to be in it?"

Leroy shrugged. He waited until the bus pulled to a stop in Windsor. As Richard swung out of his seat and lumbered up the aisle, Leroy shouted after him, "I'm in it too."

He slid down in his seat, closed his eyes, and didn't open them until the bus started to pull away. Then he glanced quickly out of the window.

Richard was leaning against the telephone pole at the bus stop, staring at the bus and shaking his head.

Leroy reached into the torn seat, found his extra pencil, and snapped it in half. He really wanted to jump off the bus and head for the mountain.

Instead he got off the bus at his own stop and spent the next hour practicing "Drums."

Now he thought about the music as he started to get dressed for the recital. "*Bom, bom, bom,*" he said under his breath, trying to remember how the notes went. "*Bomp, de bomp.*" He pulled on his shirt, trying to play an invisible piano at the same time. *Bom. Bom. Bomp.*

He couldn't remember the rest. If only Aunt Louise would let them use their music. Suppose he couldn't remember tonight? *Bomp de bomp de bump.* There it was. He'd remember.

He finished getting dressed and went downstairs. His mother and father were all dressed up. It seemed strange to see his father in a suit and his mother with earrings.

"Let's go," he muttered and followed them out the door and into the car.

Lights from the church hall spilled out onto the snow as they pulled into the parking lot. "You'll be wonderful," his mother said. They got out of the car and hurried into the back of the hall. His father patted his shoulder. "Don't worry," he told Leroy. "It's not the end of the world if you make a couple of mistakes."

The auditorium was almost full. Even Poopsie Pomeranz was there. The doctor had taken her cast off this afternoon and her grandmother had brought her home so she could come to the recital.

Leroy hurried up the side aisle and went into the small room next to the stage. Aunt Louise was dressed in lace from head to toes. Pale green. And she had about a thousand diamonds on. She kept clapping her hands but she couldn't seem to get everybody to stop running around.

Finally she stamped her foot and everyone stopped talking and stood still. "Now," she said, fanning her face with a program, "we'll line up and march into the hall. Then we will sit like ladies and gentlemen. I will announce each child. When I do, you will go to the front of the stage, bow, play your solo, bow again, and go back to your seat."

Bow. Leroy grit his teeth. He wouldn't bow for a million dollars.

"Don't forget to bow," Aunt Louise said. "I'd hate to remind you in front of everybody."

Leroy lined up behind Mitchell and stared at the back of his head on the way into the auditorium. There was a row of gold metal chairs set up on the stage. The line clumped up the three steps and sat down.

Leroy looked to see where his mother and father were sitting. After a minute he spotted them toward the back. They were sitting with Richard's parents. Leroy's father looked as if he were going to fall asleep any minute.

Leroy looked at Richard. He was sitting there, down in the front row, eating a package of peanuts and punching Tracy on the shoulder. Both of them were laughing and pointing at Elaine.

Leroy tried to think about ice fishing. Gideon's friends would be arriving at Mrs. Clausson's boarding-house tomorrow morning and the ice-fishing business would begin. But Leroy couldn't concentrate on the worms. He tried to remember how the notes went. *Bom, bom, bom.* He couldn't seem to remember how the music ended. He could feel his hands getting gooey.

Aunt Louise swished up to the front of the stage. "Ladies and gentlemen," she said in a loud voice.

"Welcome to our first annual recital. And tonight, our opening performance will be by Miss . . ." She paused, then began again in a loud voice, "Miss E-laine Everhart."

Elaine marched to the center of the stage. She was a sight. All ribbons and pink shiny stuff. She was giggling all over the place. She held her dress out and made some kind of a silly bow, then sat down at the piano and began to sing.

She sounded like Fumbles when he howled at a woodchuck.

Next to Leroy, Mitchell was shaking his head. "Would you believe it?" he whispered. "How would you like to be stuck with a pinhead like that for a sister?"

Leroy looked at him. Then he looked back at Elaine and shuddered. The thought of having Elaine for a sister was revolting. He stared down at his knees. He still couldn't remember the end of his piece. *Bom. Bom. Bom.* Or was it *bom, bing, bom.* He hoped it would come to him when he played the piece through.

Ann Marie Abbott, one of the kids from Windsor, was next. She made only one mistake, but it was right in the beginning. Richard started to laugh again. The lady in the row in back of him made a big shushing noise.

While Leroy listened to everyone else play, he practiced the beginning of his piece in his head. Finally only he and Mitchell were left. He glanced at the audience again. Richard was holding his empty peanut wrapper up in the air, trying to get out the last bit of salt, and Tracy was twirling her braids around her head.

Then it was his turn. Mitchell would be last. Leroy marched up to the piano. Aunt Louise cleared her throat, reminding him to bow. He jerked his head up and down a couple of times and wiped his hands on the sides of his pants.

Then he sat down and began to play. At first it sounded good. Smooth and loud. Out of the corner of his eye he looked down at Tracy and Richard. But now the whole auditorium was nothing but a blur. Quickly he looked back at the keys, terrified that he'd make a terrible-sounding mistake.

When he got toward the end, he played a little faster. He was still not sure of the ending and figured if he raced along it would suddenly work itself out.

It didn't.

He played the last note and started the whole thing over so quickly that nobody could tell he had made a mistake. He looked at the audience again. His father was sitting back in his seat, mouth open, fast asleep. His mother was nodding her head in time with the music. She was smiling a little, looking proud.

But Aunt Louise had sat up a little straighter. There were two bright spots of color in her cheeks.

She knew exactly what had happened.

By the time Leroy had started "Drums in the West" for the third time, he was getting a little desperate. He played as fast as he could. It was really getting late.

Suddenly behind him there was a crash. He sneaked

Behind him there was a crash.

a quick look. Mitchell had staggered to his feet. As Leroy watched, he fell on the floor in a dead faint.

Leroy played two more notes, then stood up and bowed.

But no one had noticed. Everyone was rushing up on the stage to see what had happened to Mitchell.

"Oxygen," Mitchell moaned, picking his head up off the floor. "Give me oxygen."

Everyone was milling around. "Give the boy air," someone yelled.

"How about some water?" someone else said.

Aunt Louise looked around. "Leroy," she said, "get me a glass of water, please."

Leroy went into the little room in back of the stage. There was a sink on one side of the room. A dusty cup with a dead fly in the bottom stood on the counter. Leroy turned the cup upside down to get rid of the fly, then turned on the water.

He couldn't believe it. He was saved. If Mitchell hadn't fainted, he'd probably be playing "Drums in the West" for the rest of the night.

He filled the cup, then went back onto the stage. By this time Mitchell was sitting up. "Take me outside," he said in a weak voice.

"Here," Leroy said, handing him the cup.

Mitchell took a sip, then looked down at the dirty cup. "Yucks," he said in a perfectly normal voice. Then he pushed the cup back into Leroy's hand and staggered to his feet. Aunt Louise looked as if she wanted to strangle him. "Right in the middle of everything," she muttered as she took him by the arm and marched him out the door.

Leroy stared after Mitchell suspiciously. Everyone else was whispering. "The poor child," Leroy's mother said. "I guess the excitement was just too much for him."

Leroy narrowed his eyes. Poor kid, nothing. Mitchell was faking. He was good at it, Leroy admitted to himself. But definitely faking.

He wondered why.

Because Mitchell had to be good at everything, he thought, answering his own question. And maybe he found out he wasn't so good after all. Maybe he had heard Leroy playing "Drums in the West" and figured that his violin piece was pretty stinky after all.

He jumped as he felt his mother's hand on his shoulder. "Time to go home," she said.

"Yes," said his father, yawning a little, "it looks as if the recital is over."

CHAPTER 14

The next morning when Leroy awoke, the wind was howling. The windowpanes were rattling and the sky was gray. It was probably going to snow. He lay in bed, moving his feet around to feel the warmth of the blanket and grinned as he thought of last night's recital.

Now that it was over, he was beginning to feel a little differently about the whole piano business. He had played pretty well. Except for the ending, of course, but Aunt Louise was the only one who knew about that. And in all the excitement she'd probably forgotten all about it. By next year he'd be playing really terrific stuff. Much better than Mitchell.

He put his legs over the side of the bed. Yes, old Mitchell was probably the world's worst musician. And he had chickened out when he had to play in front of everybody last night.

He stretched. Today was the day that the ice fishermen were coming. He pulled on his jeans and went downstairs to the kitchen.

His father was sitting at the table having breakfast.

He looked up when Leroy came in. "You're up early this morning," he said.

"I'm going to sell some bait," Leroy said. "And do some ice fishing at the same time. Do you mind if I borrow your auger?"

His father stood up. "Let me get it for you."

They went into the storeroom and turned on the light. The big yellow auger, looking like a giant corkscrew, was leaning against the wall behind some boxes. His father pulled the boxes away and dragged it out. "It's not that heavy," he said, "but it's kind of bulky. Are you sure you'll be able to manage to cut a hole in the ice with it? I can't help you today. I have to work."

Leroy nodded, taking the auger. It was about as high as his waist. Last year it had seemed much bigger.

"Don't forget the skimmer," said his father, reaching for the plastic spoon that was hanging on the wall. "You'll need it to get the slush out of the hole."

They went back into the kitchen, his father shaking his head. "Too bad I can't go with you. With all this overtime, I probably won't get out on a Saturday all winter." He picked up his teacup. "Mitchell going with you?"

Leroy nodded.

"He's never been ice fishing before, has he?"

Leroy shrugged. "I guess not."

"He probably doesn't even have a pole."

"Maybe not," Leroy said, thinking that maybe Mitchell wouldn't hang around after they had sold the worms.

Leroy's father went back into the storeroom. "I know what we'll do," he said when he came out. He was carrying his rod. "We'll let him use mine."

Leroy gulped. "That's really a terrific pole."

His father smiled. "It isn't doing me a bit of good hanging there in the storeroom. I'd like to think that someone was out there on the ice tomorrow, enjoying it." He put the rod next to the door with the auger and the skimmer. "Don't forget to bundle up," he told Leroy. "And have a good breakfast before you leave."

"I will," Leroy said. He turned and went back into the storeroom to get his heavy clothes, feeling as if the day was spoiled already. He had seen his father using that jigging pole so often. Now Mitchell was going to have it.

Somehow it just didn't seem right.

A little later he opened the back door and trudged around to the driveway. Tracy and Mitchell were throwing snowballs at each other on High Flats Road. As soon as they saw him, they came to meet him. "I thought you'd never get up," Mitchell said. "The ice fishermen are down at the boardinghouse having breakfast."

"How do you feel?" Leroy asked, making a face so that Mitchell would know he hadn't been fooled for one minute last night.

"Great," Mitchell said. Then he looked at Tracy. "I mean I feel a little better this morning."

He looked as healthy as a horse, Leroy thought. "How about wiping those crumbs off your mouth," he said, "and that jelly. I can see everything you had for breakfast." He handed Mitchell the box of worms. "Hold this for a second, will you? I have to get something. And be careful of those worms. That box is falling apart."

"Hurry up," Tracy said. "We have to get set up."

Leroy leaned out the door. "Hold your horses, Tracy. I have to get my fishing stuff. You don't think I'm going to hang around on the ice all day without trying to catch a perch or something, do you?"

He ran upstairs, grabbed his jigging pole, then downstairs again, tucked the rods and skimmer under his arm, and dragged the auger out the back door.

Tracy and Mitchell were staggering down High Flats Road ahead of him, carrying the box of worms between them. He caught up with them at the bridge.

"Too bad we never got that bait store finished," Mitchell said, shivering. He set the worm box down.

Tracy snorted. "Never even got it started. We'll have to work on it next summer." She scooped some snow off the iron bar of the bridge and tossed it down on the ice. "Speaking of never getting started, what happened to you last night? I thought you were dead."

Mitchell's face reddened. "No. It was just . . ."

"Well, as long as you're all right now. That's the main thing." She turned to Leroy. "You played pretty good," she said. "Loud." She nodded. "A little fast maybe."

"Drums are supposed to be fast," Leroy lied. He rubbed his hand along his father's jigging pole, then thrust it into Mitchell's hands.

"What's this?" Mitchell asked.

"My father's," Leroy said shortly. "You can use it today."

Mitchell's mouth opened. "That's really great. I'll probably catch a terrific—"

"Let's not stand around here talking," Leroy said. "I want to make a hole in the ice for myself before the fishermen get down here."

With the auger clanking behind him, he marched off the bridge. "Wait up," Tracy yelled as she and Mitchell followed. Snow was piled up high on the banks. Only the milkweed stalks and the goldenrod stuck out. They rustled in the wind. They slid down the path next to the bridge, Mitchell, almost on his seat, holding the worms.

"Be careful," Leroy said. "Treat those worms like money."

By this time Elaine was standing on top of the bridge. "Why didn't you wait for me, Mitchell?" she screamed. "Mother said I could be in the business too. *What are you doing?*"

"Get out of here," Mitchell yelled back. "Do you have to follow me all over the place?"

Leroy stopped walking. "Watch out for those worms," he yelled. He dug the point of the auger into the ice and turned the handle until he had chiseled out a neat hole. He stood back to admire it. His father or Gideon couldn't have done any better.

"Make one for me," Tracy said. "No sense my going back to get my father's."

"I'm telling Mother," Elaine shouted. She slid across the ice toward them. "You're not saving anything for

"Save me," Elaine screamed.

me to do. And then when it's time to divide up the money you'll say I can't have any."

Leroy opened his mouth. It was about time to tell Elaine that she wasn't getting one penny of this.

"You're getting to be a pain," Tracy said before he had a chance. She pulled her woolen hat over her eyebrows. "A big pain. You're not getting any money. You're just lucky we let you watch."

"I'm going to tell your mother too," Elaine said. "Leroy's the only one who's nice to me."

Leroy grinned. With the skimmer he started to skim off some of the slush that was forming in his fishing hole. Elaine would get it now, he figured. Nobody told on Tracy Matson and got away with it.

He was right.

Tracy started for Elaine. "Listen," she said. "I'll give you ten seconds to get out of here."

"Mitchell," Elaine shrieked as Tracy began to count.

"Eight . . . nine . . . ten," Tracy yelled. "Here I come, Elaine. You'd better get going."

Elaine darted toward Mitchell. "Save me," she screamed. She grabbed his arm and slid around him.

Mitchell staggered, trying to catch his balance. They watched, horrified, as the bottom of the worm box collapsed and dirt, worms, and rabbit manure fell through the hole in the ice.

CHAPTER 15

Leroy dropped down on his hands and knees and scrambled around, frantically trying to sift through the dirt that was piled up around the hole.

Mitchell leaned over next to him. He grabbed the skimmer and tried to scoop up the worms as they floated around in the slushy water.

Leroy looked around wildly. "Get me something to put these in," he yelled at Tracy.

She pulled off her hat and held it upside down so that Leroy could drop in a pair of tangled worms. Mitchell pulled up a worm on the end of the skimmer. "Frozen, I think," he said, "but usable." He tossed it over toward Tracy.

Leroy reached for another one.

Five minutes later they counted the worms in Tracy's hat. "Nineteen," Leroy said in disgust.

No one said anything. The only sound was the wind whistling around them. Gideon and his friends would be coming along any minute. Leroy wondered what they would think.

"What are we going to do?" Elaine asked. She pulled off her mitten and stuck her thumb in her mouth.

"*What are we going to do?*" Tracy screamed. "Nineteen worms. The business is over. Finished." Her eyes were narrowed almost to slits and her face was all red. "Finished," she repeated.

Elaine sniffled and began to cry. "It wasn't my fault."

Tracy stuck her hands on her hips. "It certainly was. Yours and your clumsy brother's. Leroy told him to be careful with those worms about twenty times. But Mitchell thought he was so smart." She shook her head. "Well, between the two of you, you just ruined the whole business."

Leroy blinked. It was the first time Tracy had talked to Mitchell without acting as if he were the king of High Flats. He almost felt sorry for him. Mitchell looked as if he didn't know what to do. He stood there for a minute looking down at the hole in the ice. "I guess you're right," he said finally. "It was my fault." He turned and went back toward the bridge.

As Mitchell climbed up the path, Elaine put her mitten back on. "Let's cut the worms in half," she said.

"Idiot," Tracy screamed. "You can't do that."

Leroy watched as Elaine began to cry again. He had been all set to suggest the same thing. He looked up at the goldenrod on the bank. "Maybe we could get some grubs," he said.

"Break off the pods?" Tracy frowned. "The snow must be way above our knees. Besides, there's not enough time."

"We could start the fishermen off with the worms. Then we could get some pods before they needed to bait their lines again."

Tracy nodded. She grabbed Elaine by the arm. "Stop crying," she said. She marched her over to the river-bank and pointed to a dried stalk of goldenrod halfway up the bank. "Get up there," she said. "You see that little bump on the top of that weed? That's a pod. Inside is a grub. The fishermen can use it for bait. Just snap the pod off. Get as many as you can." Tracy bent over her. "And listen, Elaine, don't mess up this time."

Elaine looked up at the bank doubtfully. "It's pretty snowy in there," she said. "Besides, I have to go to the bathroom." She scrambled away from Tracy and slid along the ice toward the bridge.

Tracy slapped her hands on the sides of her jeans. "She's not as dumb as I thought." She grinned at Leroy. "I guess we'll have to get them ourselves."

Leroy grinned back. "If she does come back," he said, "we'll have to cut her into the business, I guess." He glanced up at the bridge. "Here they come."

They watched as the first four fishermen, carrying all kinds of equipment, plodded down the path toward them. Fumbles, who had followed them down High Flats Road, stopped at the bridge and sat there watching.

"Here, Fumbles," Leroy called, but the dog looked away, pretending he hadn't heard. Fumbles hated to slide around on the ice.

Leroy called him once more, then turned back to

Tracy. By this time Gideon and the other fishermen were beginning to make holes in the ice. "Fresh worms," Tracy yelled at them. "Good and juicy."

Leroy looked down at the worms. They didn't look any too fresh. Or juicy either. But the fishermen didn't seem to notice. They grabbed up the worms, handed them a couple of dollars, and began to set up their equipment.

Leroy watched as one of them dug a hole and dropped a tip-up with its little red flag into the icy water. It was a strange-looking contraption, Leroy thought, but a great one. When a fish struck, the flag would pop up to let the fishermen know he had caught something.

"Here comes Elaine," Tracy said.

Elaine slithered across the ice toward them. She was holding something in her mitten. "I have another worm," she yelled.

"Where did you get that?" Tracy asked.

Leroy gulped. He didn't have to wait for Elaine to answer. It was Mitchell's worm she was holding out in her hand. It was dried up and brown, and still tangled in the string that Mitchell had worn around his neck.

"What do you call this mess?" Tracy asked again. She poked at the worm.

"Mitchell said he guessed you needed it more than he did."

"For what?" Tracy asked.

"Bait."

Tracy snorted. "No one wants a dead worm."

"He took it right off his neck," Elaine said.

"Is he crazy?" Tracy exploded. Then she shook her head. "Maybe it's because he was sick last night. He didn't know what he was doing."

Elaine twirled the worm around on its string. "He wasn't sick. He was making believe."

"I *knew* it," Leroy said.

"Making believe?" Tracy repeated. "You mean he didn't know how to play his piece?"

"Sure he did. But he said . . ." Elaine wrinkled her forehead trying to remember. "He said he had to stop the drums."

Leroy swallowed. Mitchell had stopped the drums all right. "Drums in the West." On purpose? To save him? He couldn't believe it. "Are you sure he said that?"

Elaine nodded.

Tracy's mouth opened. "He must have gone crazy. I guess I shouldn't have yelled at him. Where is he now?"

Elaine pointed her thumb toward Hubbell Mountain. "Up there. He said he's going to save Leroy." She put her thumb in her mouth. "Even if it kills him," she said wetly.

"I wonder what he's talking about?" Tracy asked. "We'll have to go up and find him as soon as we finish here." She waded up on the bank, sinking into the snow to her knees.

Leroy spotted a goldenrod stalk near the top of the bank. He stared at it, trying to decide whether it was worth going after. He just couldn't seem to concentrate on the bait, or the fishing. Mitchell was probably half-way up Hubbell Mountain by this time. Looking for monkeys that didn't even exist. Thinking that he might get killed and all because he believed that sooner or later the monkeys were going to kill Leroy for telling on them.

Leroy plodded up the bank next to Tracy and broke off a pod.

He asked himself why Mitchell was being so brave. "He thinks it's all his fault," he told himself out loud.

"What?" Tracy asked.

"I'm thinking about Mitchell. He thinks it's his fault about my taking piano lessons, I guess, and ruining the worm business, and maybe . . ." Leroy broke off.

Tracy was watching him.

"Who knows," he said, "he may even think it's his fault that his father isn't here anymore."

Tracy looked serious. "He sure needs a friend." She shook her head. "He wants to make friends. But I guess he doesn't know how sometimes. He tries to help every-one out."

"Some help," Leroy said, then he thought about Mitchell fainting.

Tracy looked a little embarrassed. "For the first time I know the nine times table."

"But he acts like such a big shot. And he's always got stuff all over his mouth. . . ."

"So what," Tracy said. "I can't read. And you're a pain sometimes too. You're no saint, you know."

Leroy pulled off two more pods. "You're right," he

said. "Listen, do me a favor. Keep the business going while I'm gone. I think I'd better go find Mitchell."

"I might as well. I'm soaked through anyway," she said. "Hey, look who's coming."

Leroy looked up and grinned. It was Poopsie Pomeranz, bundled up to the teeth, clumping her way down on the ice.

"I think Mitchell's life has just taken a turn for the better," he said. "Poopsie and Elaine will be just right together."

Tracy nodded. "We'll introduce them and they can pick pods for us." She leaned over closer to Leroy. "Why do you suppose Mitchell was wearing that worm around his neck anyway?"

Leroy gulped. "I'll tell you some other time. Listen, Tracy. Let me go find him." He slid across the ice and climbed the path to the bridge. "Come on, Fumbles," he yelled. "We've got to get Mitchell."

Fumbles picked himself up and trailed after Leroy as he raced down High Flats Road and plodded up Hubbell Mountain.

It was really cold. His jeans felt icy against his legs. It had started to snow, and he could just about see Mitchell's footprints ahead of him.

"Mitchell," he yelled. "Come on back." But the wind tore the words out of his mouth.

He tried to feel annoyed. He really should be down on the ice with Tracy, gathering up the pods.

But he didn't feel annoyed at all. What he felt was guilty. And mean. Tracy was right. Mitchell wasn't so bad. He wasn't great. But he wasn't nearly as bad as Leroy had been thinking. He thought back to last night. If Mitchell hadn't fainted on the floor, he would have ended up looking like a first-class idiot, not even able to finish a simple piece like "Drums in the West."

And now Mitchell was ready to kill the monkeys so they wouldn't get Leroy.

"Wait up, Mitchell," he yelled again, even though he could just about hear his own voice in the wind.

At the slate pile he stopped to catch his breath. Fumbles danced around him, playing with a stick he had found down near the bridge.

Then Leroy caught sight of Mitchell's brown leather hat. Mitchell was perched on a rock a little farther up on the mountain, waving a huge rope around half-heartedly. He looked as if he were freezing.

Fumbles spotted Mitchell at the same. He barked once and raced up the mountain with the stick in his mouth.

Mitchell must have heard something. He glanced over his shoulder, took one look at Fumbles, and tumbled off his rock into the snow. He didn't even try to stand up. He scrambled behind the rock.

Thinking this was some kind of new game, Fumbles sat down and waited for Mitchell to come out and play with him.

Leroy grinned to himself. He was glad to see that Mitchell wasn't quite as brave as he might be. He started toward the rock.

At the same time, the rope, almost as if it had a life

Mitchell looked as if he were freezing.

PATRICIA REILLY GIFF

of its own, snaked out from behind the rock. It just missed Fumbles.

Fumbles looked at Leroy and blinked.

Now Leroy could hear Mitchell. He was squeaking, "*Oh ha.* I mean, *Oh he ha.* I mean, *Ha he ha.*"

Leroy watched as the rope slowly disappeared behind the rock.

Mitchell was going to try again.

Leroy dove for Fumbles as the rope came whistling through the air and landed on them both.

"*Yeow,*" Leroy yelled.

Fumbles thought it was a great game. He rolled on top of Leroy and began to tug at the rope.

"*He he he,*" Mitchell screamed at the top of his lungs and bounded out from behind the rock. "*I've got you!*"

Leroy shook himself, trying to get Fumbles and the rope off himself. He spit out some of Fumbles's wet hair.

Mitchell's eyes opened wide. "Leroy?" he said. "Leroy?"

Leroy stood up. "It's me all right. Me and the old mountain monkey, Fumbles."

Mitchell sat down on the rock. Hard. "I knew it all the time," he said after a minute. "I was just practicing."

"Sure," Leroy said. He tried to think of something to say. He bent down and patted Fumbles. "We saved the business," he said. "With grubs. We'll need you to help get some more."

Mitchell nodded. "All right," he said. "I've been

130

looking around for the Big Ones, but I haven't seen any."

"That's why I came up here. To tell you. I don't think the monkey story is . . ." He hesitated. "Maybe they're all really dead by now. In fact I think I heard one of the fishermen say they've disappeared. Gone up north."

Mitchell sighed.

Leroy gulped, remembering back to when Richard had told him the same thing. How could he have forgotten? It hadn't been funny. It had been terrible. Really terrible.

"I was afraid," Leroy said slowly, "when the kids told me about the mountain monkeys. Scared out of my wits. I couldn't even go to sleep at night."

Mitchell ducked his head. "I know what you mean. I guess there aren't any. Are there?"

Leroy shook his head. "I'm sorry. Everybody just seems to tell that to the new kids. But . . ." He broke off and looked at Mitchell. "No one . . . no one ever went up to catch a mountain monkey before, Mitchell. Not me. Not any new kid."

Mitchell stood up and dusted the snow off his jeans. He looked at Leroy seriously. "Does that mean I'm not a new kid anymore?"

Leroy nodded. He'd have to have a little talk with Richard. He noticed that Mitchell had crumbs all over his mouth. Leroy didn't know how he managed to get his face into such a mess all the time.

"Wipe your mouth," he said automatically, thinking

that he might be able to get used to Mitchell and his messy eating habits after all. "You know," he said, "Mrs. Claycomb is right. January is a great month. You're going to love it. Gideon will probably take us skiing one of these days, and he said he's going to teach all the kids how to toboggan, and . . ."

"I bet I'm going to be good at that," Mitchell said.

Leroy sighed, "I thought you were going to say that."

"I just don't want you to think I'm a jerk or something up here in the mountains. I'm trying to learn things as fast as I can."

Leroy nodded. "I know. But right now we'd better get back down on the ice." He picked up a stick and threw it down the path for Fumbles to chase.

"How about showing me how to catch a fish?" Mitchell asked. "A perch, or something."

Leroy grinned. "Yeah. Sure. I'm good at that. Let's go. Tracy can't take care of the business by herself all day."